AGENCY

AGENCY

The thrilling story of a struggle for hearts and minds amid passions, natural disaster and human folly

MICHAEL CARY ANDERS

Copyright © 2024 Michael Cary Anders

The moral right of the author has been asserted.

Apart from any fair dealing for the purposes of research or private study, or criticism or review, as permitted under the Copyright, Designs and Patents Act 1988, this publication may only be reproduced, stored or transmitted, in any form or by any means, with the prior permission in writing of the publishers, or in the case of reprographic reproduction in accordance with the terms of licences issued by the Copyright Licensing Agency. Enquiries concerning reproduction outside those terms should be sent to the publishers.

This is a work of fiction. Names, characters, businesses, places, events and incidents are either the products of the author's imagination or used in a fictitious manner. Any resemblance to actual persons, living or dead, or actual events is purely coincidental.

Troubador Publishing Ltd
Unit E2 Airfield Business Park,
Harrison Road, Market Harborough,
Leicestershire LE16 7UL
Tel: 0116 279 2299
Email: books@troubador.co.uk
Web: www.troubador.co.uk

ISBN 978 1 80514 308 6

British Library Cataloguing in Publication Data.
A catalogue record for this book is available from the British Library.

Printed and bound by CPI Group (UK) Ltd, Croydon, CR0 4YY
Typeset in 11pt Minion Pro by Troubador Publishing Ltd, Leicester, UK

This book is dedicated to the memory of Roger James, medical doctor, poet and writer friend, whose helpful comments and suggestions upon an early draft went a long way to improving my final effort.

And so the wheel of fortune turns: some turn with it in time, and some are crushed by it, as by the hand of fate…

PROLOGUE

There is a tendency to glamorise the lives of journalists and especially those of reporters. At the same time there has always been another, apparently contradictory, tendency to vilify those whose task it is to bring the (usually) bad news. Yet the public at large generally knows little about news agencies and their important role among the mass media.

This is a story about the men and women who, round the clock, provide the unending flow of information, photos and current affairs articles that a big international news agency must supply to its clients, whether they be newspapers or broadcast media, Internet websites, or the multitude of various governmental and non-governmental bodies such as ministries, departments and specialised agencies and bureaux that exist today.

I hope I have portrayed the characters of my tale in convincing and (mostly) sympathetic manner, for they are modelled upon the generally unsung heroes and heroines of everyday working life in just such a news agency of which it was my privilege to be a part.

This is a story of disasters – both natural and man-made – of power struggles and pettiness, of romantic and sexual passions, of government-sanctioned greed and destruction, and of the triumph of collective resistance.

Those readers who have some knowledge of the field

may easily recognise the organisation on which I have loosely based this fictitious account with its fictitious characters. Most readers will, I am sure, recognise the social, political and economic forces that I have sought to portray, for they have a universal nature in this age of globalisation.

A word of warning to the reader is perhaps called for here: this story is, broadly speaking, about the class struggle. By this I do not mean to invoke any notions of faceless forces and historical inevitability. Quite the contrary, in fact. I believe the course of human events is shaped by the conscious will and decision of flesh-and-blood individuals in their various struggles for integrity, emancipation and survival.

At the risk of seeming pretentious, I have sought to portray the struggle within the fictitious news agency France-Dépêches as part of Man's search for social and economic justice and democracy amid the throes of decadent twenty-first century capitalism. That said, the book is intended to be, and pretends to be no more than, a work of light entertainment.

M.C.A.

THE MAIN CHARACTERS

(French, unless otherwise stated)

Andy Mitchell, agency journalist, later freelance, English

Cheryl Keyes, agency journalist, Canadian

Bertrand Rainier, Nairobi regional bureau chief

Gareth Galant, agency journalist, political and trade union militant

Marie-Claude Schroedinger, agency journalist, mistress of Galant

Christophe Juliet, government-placed boss of the agency, businessman

Paul Ventrex, senior agency journalist, party and trade union activist

Jean-François Cardenal, Santa de Costa regional bureau chief

Francis Renaulde, veteran journalist, deputy agency boss, replaces Juliet

Otelo Okello (Otto), journalist and lover of Cheryl, African

Njoki, lover of Andy, soon to be his wife, African

Russell McCarthy, Hong Kong regional bureau chief, management figure, American

PART ONE

CHAPTER 1

Suddenly and unexpectedly, the dusty old telex machine in a far corner of the office clattered into life.

As the apparatus, of obscure Yugoslav manufacture, began disgorging its message, Matt, one of the Nairobi bureau's local hires, walked over to the machine and peered at the faint words being laboriously printed out in irregular capital letters on a roll of shiny porridge-coloured paper. At the same time he caught the loose end of the punched tape that was emerging from one side of the machine and began to loop it into a kind of skilful double bow.

"Murumi, Omarou islands," Matt called out to Andy and Henri, the two staff correspondents of the France-Dépêches regional bureau.

The end of the message was signalled by a series of scratchy bell-tones emitted by the telex machine, after which the clattering ceased as abruptly as it had begun.

Matt deftly tore off the printed paper message and bore it over to Andy, before taking the punched tape and feeding it into another machine in order to enter the message into the bureau's computer system.

"What do you make of this?"

Andy Mitchell drew the attention of his French

colleague to the telex message that had just been handed to him by Matt. It was rare, in the twenty-first century, still to receive messages by telex, which had become the communications method of a bygone age. Very few news correspondents now sent their despatches by that means.

"Fort intéressant," (Very interesting) replied Henri after perusing the piece of paper for a few moments. *"Mais j'aime pas trop ça."* (But I don't much like it).

In the Nairobi office, staff journalists employed both English and French among themselves, but the text of the telex had tested Andy's comprehension to the limit and he'd needed Henri's opinion.

In quaint and laboured French, the message from Murumi, capital of the Omarou archipelago in the Indian Ocean, spoke of a serious and so-far-unidentified disease which had broken out on one of the islands. The outbreak had led the Omarou government to ban all sea- and air-traffic to and from the affected island of Oreli.

What the message did not say, but which its author knew perfectly well, as did both Andy and Henri, was that Oreli had two months earlier unilaterally declared its secession from the Republic of Omarou.

The disease was described as characterised by a high fever and headache accompanied by a dark rash on the chest and abdomen. After a few days the rash would give way to a painful, weeping eruption of the skin. Within a week to ten days, the patient usually died. The convoluted message gave no indication of the number of victims or the clinical nature of the disease.

After briefly discussing the information, Henri and Andy each prepared a short, factual despatch in his own working language – Henri Laborie the Frenchman in French, Andy Mitchell the Englishman in English – and each sent his copy to his respective news desk at the France-Dépêches head office in Paris.

Henri also prepared a service note for the agency's correspondent in Murumi, Omar Ali Sinbadi, thanking him for his despatch and asking a series of questions about the outbreak of the disease, stressing their interest in any additional information.

Before they had time to send the note to Murumi – it could take hours before one got through by telex, and the telephone line was more unreliable still – there came a service note from the foreign news editors-in-chief in Paris asking more questions. These were then incorporated into the note for Omar Ali.

Within half an hour of the original telex from Murumi landing in Nairobi, the French- and English-language 'news-wires' – the services received by press and broadcast media clients of France-Dépêches – were carrying a 150-word despatch reporting that an unidentified and apparently fatal disease had broken out on one of the islands of the Omarou archipelago, and that the island had been 'sealed off'.

The last paragraph of the heavily re-written despatch recalled that the affected island of Oreli had two months earlier declared its secession from the Omarou Republic.

The 'mystery disease' story, as they called it, was the last one that Andy and Henri handled before quitting the Nairobi office that evening, leaving it to the local staff to monitor the regional radios and incoming communications. Apart from that disease story, it had been a quiet day for eastern Africa and the Indian Ocean, their region.

Henri went home to his wife and child in Langata, one of the better suburbs of the Kenyan capital. Andy, who lived in Westlands and was single, headed for the bar of the Rainbow Hotel in the city centre, a favourite watering hole of his.

What the pair could not yet know was that France-Dépêches had just delivered a scoop, and that this was the start of a major running story. But when it comes to breaking news of this kind, the wire service agencies tend to be first, ahead even of the broadcast networks like CNN and the BBC.

The next day, when it came to checking the controls or logs – a system of monitoring to see which news agency had been used on which story of international interest – the world's papers were as usual full of bloody violence in Iraq and Afghanistan, revolution and civil war in the Middle East, US President Barack Obama's re-election campaign, and of course the world economic crisis…

So far as one could tell, only the African and the Indian newspapers had picked up the 'mystery disease' item. Only the Nairobi and Dar es Salaam papers had given it any prominence at all. Not even Madagascar or Mauritius picked it up – it came too late for them, perhaps – and it got just one paragraph in Mumbai (Bombay).

For the rest of the world's media, it was apparently not even worth that. For the meantime, anyway.

But by midday, Andy and Henri already had an inkling that they were maybe onto something big, when Murumi sent a new despatch. The disease had been detected elsewhere in the Omarou archipelago and the government had banned all but essential movement between the islands.

The new despatch also stated that the World Health Organization (WHO) had been notified about the disease, and that its assistance was being sought.

This time, after a swift re-write, and in Andy's case a translation, the two journalists sent their copy on to Paris marked 'urgent'. Henri also drafted a service note for Paris requesting that the Geneva bureau's attention be drawn to the story, as the WHO has its headquarters in that lakeside Swiss city.

Frustratingly, the Murumi correspondent had still not stated how many people had been infected or had died of the disease. But by a minor miracle, Henri was able to reach him by telephone later in the afternoon, and to extract from him an unofficial figure of "tens, perhaps hundreds". That information alone merited a further despatch, even though the source was not very satisfactory, because it was not attributable.

The conversation with the correspondent was difficult, and not only because the line was bad. Omar Ali appeared to be nervous, stuttering in his speech. It was not clear why, and what relation, if any, this had to the fact that the disease had apparently broken out first on Oreli, the 'secessionist' island.

Henri then sent a service note to the French- and English-language news desks, announcing that the Nairobi bureau would be filing a new story of five hundred words in the two languages about the 'mystery disease' in the Omarou archipelago that afternoon, so that clients could be advised to expect it.

About half of the story would in fact be 'background' material, but when it came to the Omarou islands there was a rich store of that. Once host to the famous pirate Captain Kidd, and a haunt of the legendary Sinbad the Sailor, the archipelago had long been known as a source of exotic spices such as vanilla and cinnamon.

In more recent times, the republic had been noted for its political instability. Presidents had been overthrown and reinstated with the help of European-led mercenary forces, who also constituted the backbone of a notoriously bloody 'presidential guard'.

Colonised by France in the nineteenth century, but staunchly Islamic in religion and culture, the islands gained their independence in 1975 – all save one island, Mayota, which in a referendum opted to remain French, to the bitter chagrin of the independent regime.

Now the inhabitants of Oreli had voted to declare their 'independence' from Murumi too, in the apparent hope of also returning to a French administration. The general explanation for this anachronism was that Oreli hoped thereby to benefit from French government subsidies, like Mayota.

While Henri and Andy were writing their scheduled story, there came on the wires a brief item datelined Geneva. The WHO confirmed that it had been notified of the epidemic of an unidentified disease in the Omarou islands.

The WHO also revealed a death toll of seventy-nine people, based on figures given by the local government, with an unknown number seriously ill. The WHO said it had advised the authorities to declare the archipelago 'under quarantine' and that a regional medical team was setting out for Murumi.

These brief but vital new facts allowed the two journalists to considerably harden up their story and hang it on an official source – important for a news agency which needs to be scrupulous in this respect.

At this point, Henri and Andy also resolved, in

view of the apparent nervousness of the correspondent in Murumi, and because much of the material in their upcoming copy was background matter or from another source, that it should not carry Omar Ali's by-line.

A service note to editors in Paris explained that the story, although datelined Murumi, should carry no by-line of authorship or the local correspondent's initials. It would be understood that the decision was probably in order to protect a local correspondent in a sensitive situation.

This sort of decision would normally have been taken by the regional bureau chief, Bertrand Rainier. However, Rainier was not in Nairobi that day. He had flown to Paris earlier in the week to attend a special two-day meeting of France-Dépêches bureau and service chiefs with the agency's new managing director.

CHAPTER 2

Gareth Galant, the agency's deputy chief of political and parliamentary news, knew that France-Dépêches was heading for a major crisis before even a word had leaked out of the meeting that the new managing director, Christophe Juliet, was having with service and bureau chiefs in the conference room of the agency headquarters in Paris's Place de l'Horloge.

A political militant and trade union leader, Galant guessed pretty much what was coming; all that lacked were the details of where and how the axe was going to fall.

Christophe Juliet, the man chosen by the government to head France-Dépêches, had a reputation as one of a new breed of managers. It had been the same story at all three companies he had previously headed in the last seven years: radical rationalisation and restructuring, resulting in the disappearance of hundreds of jobs, in efforts to turn financial losses into profits.

Now the man was going to apply his methods to France-Dépêches, with an important difference: this would be the first time that Juliet had operated outside the private sector, for France-Dépêches had always enjoyed a protected and special semi-public status.

Juliet had been designated by a new right-wing government. In reporting his appointment, the French business press noted the man's close personal links to the finance minister, Jean-Olivier Delachasse. That the 'new broom' boss had no previous experience of working in the news media was seemingly overlooked.

Quoting sources 'close to the minister', the reports said Juliet's task at France-Dépêches would be to phase out rapidly the government subsidies which had been keeping the agency financially solvent for the last four decades and to find ways of making France-Dépêches attractive for a part-privatisation. To make the agency profitable for private interests, in short.

The managing director's meeting with service and bureau chiefs was on the Tuesday and the Wednesday of that week. At the joint request of trade union officials representing all the agency's journalists and other employees, Juliet had agreed to meet with a trade union delegation for one hour at midday Thursday to outline his intentions.

Anticipating the worst, Galant convened a special meeting of all the agency's Democratic Union (DU) sections for Thursday evening, and proposed to leaders of the other, rival trade unions at France-Dépêches the holding of a mass meeting of all staff who were able to attend for Friday at 1400 hours in the main Paris newsroom. The other three trade unions represented in the agency agreed to Galant's proposal.

The General Union (GU), at the instigation of senior journalist Paul Ventrex, also called a special meeting of all its members for Thursday evening, in parallel with the meeting of Galant's DU. The purpose in both cases was to inform and galvanise their respective members and prepare the ground for Friday's mass meeting.

Galant and the more perspicacious of the other local officials also took the trouble at this point of informing their respective head offices that a crisis was in the offing at the agency and that their assistance might be necessary.

There was suddenly a new tension in the air at France-Dépêches headquarters, in contrast to the usual dreary gloom that pervaded the grey six-storey concrete office block erected on the south side of the Place de l'Horloge, opposite the mock-Grecian temple of the former Paris Stock Exchange.

* * *

As scheduled, at midday Thursday, Managing Director and Chief Executive Officer Christophe Juliet, flanked by his deputy Francis Renaulde, received representatives of the journalists' and other employees' unions in his penthouse-style office on the top floor of the agency building.

The boss's office was well-situated. Looking out north through its large picture windows, one could clearly see at a few miles' distance the white round-topped towers of the church of Sacré Coeur on the hilltop of Montmartre.

Foreign tourists generally admire this edifice, notwithstanding its slight resemblance to a vulgar wedding-cake ornament. Few of them ever learn that it was consecrated by a Church and State grateful to God for the bloody crushing of the Paris Commune in 1871.

Juliet said he would try to sum up in an hour his two-day meeting with the agency's two dozen or so bureau and service chiefs. No decisions had yet been taken, he stressed. That would be up to a meeting of the agency's administrative board, to be held in three weeks' time. For the meantime, the plan he intended to put before that meeting had yet to be finalised.

"Indeed," he said, "I hope for useful, constructive input from the agency's trade unions."

But Juliet stressed that the principles and broad lines of his 'action plan' were already established. "And I believe," he went on, "that these principles and broad lines of action have been accepted by the vast majority of our bureau and service chiefs.

"Our target is to reduce to zero level all direct and indirect government subsidies by the end of next year" – a period of less than fifteen months. "The agency will in future have to find or generate its own funds for investment in new technology and new areas of activity.

"The agency also needs absolutely to rein in labour costs," the new boss added in the next breath.

In view of the difficulty the agency would in its present form have in raising the investment needed over the next few years, and because the government was no longer prepared to underwrite the agency's increasingly large annual deficit, or to privilege France-Dépêches over its rivals when it came to taking its services in ministries and embassies, a basic restructuring was called for.

"What will this restructure entail?" one of the union delegates asked.

The new managing director sought the most neutral of tones and terms in his reply.

"After the necessary groundwork, we envisage the transformation of France-Dépêches into a public limited company, with up to 49% of the capital being made available to outside investors. The government will retain a controlling share."

"But what about the agency's founding charter?" asked one of the other delegates. "As you well know, Mr Juliet, the charter specifies that the agency must not fall under the influence or control of any group or interests."

The managing director was unable to prevent himself sounding smug. He had been expecting that question.

"Of course, an Act of Parliament will be necessary," he said in his patrician drawl. "But I think you can take it for granted that this government is aware of what needs to be done with France-Dépêches and has the necessary means at its disposal."

This could have simply been an allusion to the large majority the new government disposed of in the National Assembly, which would allow it to amend the charter with relative ease. But was it perhaps a boast of some occult power within the State?

"The prime minister's office, the foreign ministry and the finance ministry will each continue to have a representative on the new board of management as they do at present," Juliet thought fit to add.

"What about the French press interests in the agency?" asked Paul Ventrex. "Will the press barons finally be made to pay a proper price for the agency's services?"

This was an old bone of contention. The Parisian and French provincial press groups represented on the present board had for years steadfastly blocked any significant increase in the price of their subscriptions to the France-Dépêches news-wires.

While the agency's foreign clients for the English, Spanish and other language wires paid competitive but realistic prices, much of the French media received the France-Dépêches wires 'on the cheap'.

Juliet had a glib but revealing response ready for this more-or-less rhetorical question from Ventrex.

"The French national and provincial press representatives whom we have sounded out understand the need for change at France-Dépêches. We hope – indeed, we expect – them to be among the investors in the new entity when the capital is opened up to the public."

Gareth Galant interjected at this point.

"You spoke just there of 'opening the capital up to the public', but what we are talking about is bringing in private, commercial interests, isn't it? If shares are put up for sale, any bank, trust or investment fund could buy into France-Dépêches, right?

"And so far," Galant added, "you have said nothing about how your plans will affect the people who work for the agency."

"As regards your first point, I have already said that the government will retain a controlling interest," the managing director replied.

"As to the impact on journalists and other employees of the agency, we – France-Dépêches management and our partners in government – we have identified a paramount need to bring down the overall cost of the payroll.

"We naturally hope that this can be achieved through voluntary departures, early retirement, non-replacement of staff who leave for other reasons and measures such as the closure of some provincial or overseas offices. We also intend to divest ourselves of some activities, and we will be out-sourcing certain ancillary services… "

Galant again interrupted the managing director.

"How many jobs would be lost under your plan, according to you, Mr Juliet?"

"The measures that we have identified as desirable or necessary will according to our best estimates result in the probable reduction of about 550 editorial posts and that of 150 employees in ancillary services," replied Juliet in the most neutral and measured tone that he could manage.

Thirty seconds of dead silence followed. Some of the union officials looked at each other in search of reaction or guidance.

"Of course there will be a certain number of job creations. We intend greatly to expand sales of specialised services over the Internet to non-media clients, and there will also be investment in a video-news service, probably in a joint venture with another partner," the managing director added.

"I obviously can't give any figures at this point, but there will be significant job creations."

Although the union representatives had expected the worst, they were still stunned. Seven hundred jobs, out of a total salaried workforce around the world of about 2,000! More than a third of the France-Dépêches workforce!

Juliet went on at some length about the potential of the Internet for France-Dépêches. He talked of "using modern information technology to bring news content to clients' desk-tops", and employed much technical jargon.

"I know it is hard for you, gentlemen," – there were no ladies among the six-member union delegation – "but there it is. France-Dépêches has to move with the times. It is my task to help ensure that it does.

"And now, if you will excuse me, I have another appointment. Perhaps you would like us to meet again next week, when we can discuss some details of matters that concern you."

Deputy Managing Director Francis Renaulde, a respected veteran journalist of the agency, had said not a word during the encounter.

None of the union officials troubled to reply to the managing director's parting invitation. They simply looked at each other absent-mindedly, each thinking about the terms in which he would be reporting back to his members and what course to follow now.

Some of them went straight to the agency canteen, driven by the automatism of sheer habit, others went to one or other of the busy cafés and restaurants situated around the Place de l'Horloge.

Managing Director Christophe Juliet, for his part,

took a chauffeur-driven car to the Quai de Bercy where he was going to lunch with an old friend from his student days and partner in earlier business ventures, Jean-Olivier Delachasse, recently elevated to the post of finance minister.

* * *

Although it was already October, Paris was still warm and sunny. As afternoon turned to evening and a magnificent blood-orange sunset washed across the Paris sky like a Cézanne painting, Gareth Galant informed members of the Democratic Union that same day of what the managing director had said.

The union meeting, held in a drab basement room of the France-Dépêches building, was attended by less than thirty people. These included a number of non-journalists organised within the DU: messengers and drivers, secretaries from personnel, clerks from the accounts department, as well as journalists.

They all listened attentively to Galant. An unusually handsome, if slightly effeminate man, Galant had the Byronic looks of a nineteenth century English poet: he had youthful charm, thanks to a shy smile and a quick wolfish grin. On most days he looked nearer thirty-five than his true forty-seven years old, if you overlooked his tobacco-stained teeth.

Women loved the way his dark curly hair fell over his

high pale forehead, and some must have imagined being kissed by his full red lips. In that very room, there were several women ready to fall in love with him, and at least one who most definitely already was.

Marie-Claude Schroedinger, a devoted union activist and political militant, was having a discreet affair with Galant, a married man. Possibly it was the strains of the affair which were responsible for the lines that had recently appeared on the face of this sad-eyed but ravishingly beautiful red-haired madonna.

Marie-Claude, who wrote for the agency on education and youth affairs, sat on the right of Galant at the meeting, and took notes as he and others spoke. She herself said not a word. Marie-Claude was secretary of the France-Dépêches cell of Workers Power, a Trotskyist group of which Galant was also an active member.

"Colleagues, there is no doubt in my mind," Galant began. "This new managing director's so-called action plan is going to lead to the worst crisis that the agency has ever known, for there is no way that any trade union can accept such job losses.

"And there is no way," he stressed with vehemence, "that any journalists' union worthy of the name can accept the scrapping of the France-Dépêches founding charter which guarantees the agency's independence."

Galant added that in his personal opinion, it was also

not a foregone conclusion that parliament would vote the necessary change, notwithstanding Juliet's apparent confidence and the support his 'action plan' evidently had in government circles.

The legislative timetable was already overloaded, and by no means all of the Members of Parliament of the right-wing majority would be ready to sacrifice the agency's independence, he explained.

"But in any event, this plan must be rejected *en bloc*, as it is entirely non-negotiable. Juliet and the government are simply going to have to be forced to withdraw it. And that means using every legitimate means possible, up to and including an all-out strike."

Not that this meant they should immediately brandish the strike threat, but they should understand the situation, Galant added. "But I think nothing less than the real threat of a strike will in the end shift the position of this managing director and this government."

As to any misgivings about the plan among 'the middle-management', he predicted that in the main the bureau and service chiefs, and many of their deputy heads too, could not be expected to put up any real resistance.

"It will be up to the unions and members of staff to stand firm and united. On that condition, this is a fight we can win. The real danger in this situation will come, I think, from inside one of the other journalists' unions.

"It's there that Juliet can expect to find useful support for a change in the agency's charter, which would open the door for privatisation."

In answer to a question, Galant made clear that he did not fear any such 'treachery' from the General Union under the leadership of Paul Ventrex, but rather from one of the smaller, supposedly independent, unions.

"Can I take it that we all agree that the Democratic Union position at tomorrow's mass meeting must be complete rejection of the 'action plan', which must be withdrawn unconditionally before there can be any discussion or negotiation about the future of the agency?" he concluded.

There was an immediate murmur of assent.

"Everyone in favour?"

More murmurs.

"Anyone against?"

Silence.

"No? Thank you, colleagues. Everybody, please, tomorrow at 1400 hours on the third floor."

Around the same time, in a similar basement room, Paul Ventrex addressed a meeting of General Union members. The room was packed with at least fifty people. Most of them seemed to know already what the managing director had told the union delegates at midday, but Paul gave them an abbreviated version anyway.

"This plan is totally unacceptable," Ventrex declared. He contrived to add, however, that it was somehow all the more unacceptable in that the unions had been in no way consulted prior to the drawing up of the 'action plan'.

"Can we take it that the General Union will be calling for withdrawal of the plan at tomorrow's mass meeting?" asked someone.

"You most certainly can," Ventrex thundered back. "We will be fighting for everyone's job."

"And will you reject any privatisation?" asked the same person.

"Yes, of course," Ventrex bellowed. "As I said, we will be demanding that the managing director withdraw his plan. We will be saying so at the general assembly, and that's what I will be saying to him personally when the unions meet with him again next week."

Asked what he thought the position of the other unions was, he said: "I can only hope that they will be as firm in their opposition to the plan as we are." He then added: "I see no reason at this point to suspect that the Democratic Union are any less than 100% opposed to the plan."

The last remark was not lost on those who knew the rivalry between Ventrex and Galant. The latter had been in the General Union before quitting a few years previously to help build a Democratic Union journalists' section at France-Dépêches.

Ventrex, like his prominent journalist father before him, had been a General Union and a Socialist Party activist most of his adult life. Intelligent, and a powerful orator, he was also an inveterate master of wheeler-dealing and intrigue.

He had been on close terms with the previous managing director, sharing the latter's taste for copious late-night dinners and expensive wines, and was on familiar terms with a number of senior Socialist Party figures.

A sharp-tongued and choleric man now in his late fifties, he spent long hours at the agency, and appeared to have no private life. The recent change at the head of the agency and the impending crisis threatened to put paid to his hopes of becoming director of news before he reached retirement age.

Indeed, he could not now be sure even of keeping his position as head of the French home news service, for Juliet was unlikely to take kindly to such opposition from someone regarded as holding a management position.

CHAPTER 3

For most of the agency staff in Paris and abroad, this October Friday morning was much like any other working day, despite the rumours and whispers surrounding the two-day meeting earlier in the week between bureau and service chiefs and the new managing director, and despite some well-informed reports in the French daily press.

But the announcement of a mass meeting in the main editorial room on the third floor was not unexpected either. Most Paris staff had already known something was afoot involving the future of the agency. The to-ing and fro-ing of trade union officials and senior managers with set, purposeful expressions in recent days had been testimony to that.

First *Libération* and, a few hours later, *Le Monde*, that day each carried articles on the theme 'Shake-up at France-Dépêches'. Both newspapers said a part-privatisation within the next two years was envisaged, and that 'up to 750' job losses were envisaged. It appeared that the same source or sources had inspired the articles of both newspapers.

Both papers carried two new nuggets of information in their reports. These said that the agency's photo archives were to be sold to the Telepresse empire of Italian press magnate and politician Salvi Burlesco, while a planned video-news venture was to be a partnership with

Robert Murphy's MediaNews International and mainland Chinese interests.

Despite all this, the day still began according to normal routine in the Place de l'Horloge. Thus the daily morning editorial conference took place as usual under the chairmanship of the director of news.

And as usual, there was a 'post mortem' of how the agency had fared in the controls compared to its main Anglo-American rivals, Amalgamated Press and Beckers, on the big stories of the last twenty-four hours. That is to say, there was an analysis of the relative performances of the agencies: which had been favoured on which story by which media, and the possible reasons for this.

The editorial executives attending the conference also identified which were the current and upcoming stories for the immediate period ahead, and typically there might also be discussion of where special correspondents were needed, and which ones could be recalled, what special arrangements would be necessary for upcoming events such as a summit meeting, and so on and so forth.

Despite the efforts of everyone to maintain an air of normalcy, there was a stiffness and formality in the exchanges on this Friday morning. The business of the day was expedited with unusual alacrity and absence of criticism, positive or negative. The 'action plan' and the imminent mass meeting had evidently rendered the editorial chiefs cautious in their expression.

* * *

At 1406 hours, an elderly trade union delegate coughed into a hand-held microphone and called the assembly to order, although people were still arriving in the main editorial room on the third floor. Some came from elsewhere in the building, some had sacrificed part of their day off to return to the office, some even came from offices in the provinces.

For those staff far away or abroad, a special radio-telephone link had been set up to allow them to follow the proceedings.

"Colleagues…" began the elderly journalist. Clearing his throat again, he explained that the four main unions had agreed that their respective spokespersons would speak for an initial maximum of fifteen minutes each, that he himself would preside, and that after the first round of four interventions, the debate would be open for everyone.

"Is that agreed, colleagues?"

A broad rumble of assent signalled that the meeting could now begin.

Ventrex was the first to speak, on behalf of the General Union sections, and gave a succinct outline of Managing Director Christophe Juliet's 'action plan'. The trade unions had not been in any way consulted before it had been presented, he stressed, adding that all sections of the GU –

journalists, admin staff, technical and maintenance – were united in their opposition to the plan.

He proposed that the unions organise a joint deputation to the parliamentary leaders of the main political parties to seek their support for opposition to the 'action plan' if Juliet refused to back down.

Next came Gareth Galant, who made a vibrant appeal for a united front of opposition to the plan by all the unions and all staff members of the agency.

"The 'action plan' must be withdrawn. It simply is not negotiable, because if it were applied, it would mean the total destruction of the agency as we know it. The key question now is unity!"

The spokespersons for the two less important unions also declared their total opposition to the 'action plan' before the debate was thrown open to the floor.

Now, for all their supposed worldliness, journalists can be remarkably naïve when it comes to their own affairs, or so it seems. Thus several speakers wondered whether there might not be some good in the managing director's 'action plan'. Not the job losses, of course, or the danger of a loss of independence. But the agency had to modernise and take advantage of the 'digital revolution' to find new markets, did it not?

And how independent could the agency be, or seem

to be, if it continued to rely on French government finance?

One or two speakers even suggested that now was indeed the time to change the founding charter of France-Dépêches, precisely to enable it to attract alternative sources of funding.

"In the final analysis, we have to compete just like everyone else in the world market for information, which is a commodity as well as a service," said one anglophone free-marketeer and stocks and bonds specialist from the economic news department. "I don't see how we can be an exception to the laws of the market."

Others warned of the perilous political situation in which the agency found itself after the recent change of government and change of managing director.

"Christophe Juliet is the placeman of this government. He's a close associate of the finance minister. If we fight him and his 'action plan', we have to understand that we will in fact be fighting the government," observed a member of the foreign and diplomatic service.

Others still by their interventions showed just how divided and even confused the personnel were over the implications of the 'action plan'.

Far from being politicised, probably less than half of those present at the mass meeting were even paid-up trade union members. Moreover, even some of the elected union officials appeared ambivalent in their positions.

Sensing a potentially dangerous drift in the debate, Paul Ventrex seized the microphone again.

"Colleagues," he began in stentorian tone, "this mass meeting has not been called in order to take any decisions. Your trade union officials are reporting back to you on the basis of what Mr Juliet told us of his 'action plan' when he called us in yesterday, which he was bound by the law to do. We will be meeting with him again early next week.

"However, for the sections of the General Union, this so-called action plan is entirely unacceptable, and that is what we for our part will be telling him next week," Ventrex added.

He handed the microphone back to the chairman of the meeting, who then called on Galant.

"I can assure you, colleagues, that Juliet's 'action plan' is entirely unacceptable to all the Democratic Union sections of France-Dépêches. Our position is that it must be withdrawn. There is absolutely no way DU can accept any job losses. And we will fight any attempt to privatise the agency.

"The founding charter must also be defended at all costs," Galant concluded.

He had made a rousing bid to rally the meeting to a

position of implacable opposition to the Juliet plan, while knowing full well that by no means all staff members shared his view.

However, after Gareth Galant's brief but eloquent words, other more ambiguous views got short shrift, at least that day, and the assembly began to break up.

The mass meeting had lasted for some fifty minutes, during which time news stories had been coming in thick and fast from all over the world. A back-log of all but the most urgent copy had started to build up while news editors and sub-editors were distracted by the mass meeting held in the main news-room.

CHAPTER 4

It was now nearly a week since France-Dépêches had broken the 'mystery disease' story and the provisional death toll on the Omarou archipelago was well beyond three hundred, according to unofficial estimates.

A team from the World Health Organization had arrived in Murumi and its sole brief communiqué since described the disease as a 'suppurating fever'. One WHO source spoke of a 'viral plague'.

The WHO had given no indication so far of the clinical nature of the disease, how it was transmitted or what similarities it might bear to existing diseases known in that part of the world, such as dengue fever, *chikungunya* or so-called Rift Valley disease.

But in view of its rapid spread and the high rate of mortality, the authorities felt bound to act firmly. All but the most essential traffic between the archipelago and the rest of the world was now officially banned on the advice of the WHO.

In reality, of course, such a strict quarantine was difficult to enforce. The islands had many small natural harbours which fishing boats or small cargo vessels and passenger ferries could and did still use. There was also a complete lack of coordination between the different authorities on the islands.

While the Islamic republic government in Murumi claimed jurisdiction over the whole of the archipelago, the island of Mayota was still officially a French overseas territory and, as already noted, Oreli where the disease was first reported had recently unilaterally declared its independence.

Meanwhile, the first suspected cases of the disease had been reported on the African mainland – in the Kenyan port city of Mombasa, in or near Lamu further to the north on the Indian Ocean coast, and possibly in Somalia too.

At the France-Dépêches regional bureau in Nairobi, Andy Mitchell and Henri Laborie had been making the most of the story and were now turning in three scheduled 500-word stories per day on latest developments concerning the 'mystery tropical disease'.

Here's how a typical example read at this stage:

WHO mute as mystery malady toll hits 300

MURUMI, 12 October – World Health Organization officials remained tight-lipped regarding a fatal mystery disease which has claimed at least 300 lives on the Indian Ocean islands of Omarou and is now believed to have spread to the East African mainland.

They have given few details or description of the 'suppurating fever' but have advised local authorities to restrict all traffic to and from the archipelago to a strict minimum pending a first report by a WHO team despatched to Murumi, the Omarou capital, earlier this week.

According to unconfirmed reports, the disease has spread to the East African coast. Kenyan newspapers have reported a death in the port of Mombasa and another on the island of Lamu, near the border with Somalia, from an apparently similar mystery disease.

The disease, described by one WHO source as a 'viral plague', was first reported on the island of Oreli, part of the Indian Ocean Omarou archipelago, some three weeks ago. Oreli declared its independence from the Omarou government in Murumi on 15 August.

The disease is characterised by a high fever and headache accompanied by a dark rash on the chest and abdomen, according to local sources.

After a few days the rash gives way to a painful, weeping eruption of the skin, and within a week or ten days, the patient usually dies, the sources said.

No official figures are currently available for the death toll to date, but local sources have spoken of at least 300.

A WHO team despatched to Murumi...

With the other news from the region – riots in western Kenya, a rebel attack in northern Uganda, drought, famine and civil war in Sudan – Andy and Henri had been kept busy over the last few days ensuring that the agency stayed ahead of the competition on the 'mystery disease' story.

The pace was now about to quicken. The WHO team was returning from the islands and had scheduled a press conference for the following day at 1700 hours (1400 GMT) in Nairobi.

Fresh news on the story had so far been sparse. But the official death toll announced by the WHO team as it left Murumi, based on figures collated with the local authorities, was now up to at least 373 dead in the space of three weeks since the first outbreak was registered, with a still unclear number of sick, infected victims.

Henri and Andy were also now in direct competition with their counterparts in the Kenyan capital – that is to say, the reporters from the two big Anglo-American news agencies, Amalgamated News and Beckers.

* * *

The WHO news conference was held at the United Nations offices some twenty miles upcountry, well outside the town of Nairobi, and precious minutes were lost as the pair of France-Dépêches reporters hesitated before one of them quit the room to telephone a short urgent paragraph on the new death toll by satellite telephone link, after efforts to send by laptop computer via the agency wires and public Internet both failed.

One of them then drove back to the office to write a full story while the other stayed at the press conference, occasionally dictating further short paragraphs by phone to a local staffer in the Nairobi bureau.

Up until now France-Dépêches, which was the only international agency to have a local correspondent in Murumi, had been consistently first with the latest on the 'mystery disease' story.

This time, however, the French agency came in third place with the urgent 'flash' to clients giving the new death toll, even if it was a question of being only some ten or twelve minutes behind the other two.

Poor organisation as well as technical problems caused the delay, which was compounded by the confusion of working in two languages, French and English, because in Paris they hadn't immediately known whether to translate the urgent news-flash.

A contributing factor too, perhaps, was the continued absence of the regional bureau chief. For unknown personal reasons, Bertrand Rainier had still not returned to Nairobi after the meeting of bureau and service chiefs in Paris the previous week with the agency's new managing director.

"Woman trouble," Andy cheekily surmised before his office colleagues.

It would normally have been Rainier's task to ensure a coordinated coverage of the news conference.

Apart from the new official death toll, the WHO team confirmed that the disease was characterised by a high fever and headache accompanied by a dark rash on the chest and abdomen. After a few days the rash would give way to a painful, weeping eruption of the skin. Within a week or ten days of becoming ill, the patient usually died.

The manner of infection was not clear: whether the vector was a kind of mosquito, or contaminated water, or whatever.

The disease appeared to be always fatal, for the medical team said that while they had found numerous people ill with the disease, neither they nor the local authorities had been able to point to a case of anyone contracting it and later recovering.

The disease appeared unrelated to any other known malady. It was definitely not related to Ebola fever, the WHO team leader added in answer to a reporter's question.

The WHO team had left one of their number in Murumi to monitor the situation, the others were returning directly to Geneva to make a fuller report there, the press conference heard.

It had not been possible for the team to confirm that the same disease had broken out in Mombasa and in Lamu. "But judging by the descriptions of the symptoms it unfortunately seems quite possible," the head of the medical team said.

The enduring political chaos in Somalia made any verification regarding the disease there virtually impossible, he indicated in answer to another question.

The WHO doctor, a tropical diseases specialist, said: "We regard the situation as quite worrying." But he declined to make any prognosis regarding the spread of this new 'viral plague'.

According to the Kenyan press reports, a dockworker in Mombasa and a sailor who had recently returned to his home in Lamu had both died in the last week after suffering from a similar-sounding 'mystery disease'.

CHAPTER 5

Andy Mitchell was in a rueful mood after the WHO press conference, knowing that his anglophone colleagues on the English news desk in Paris had been annoyed and frustrated at receiving an urgent flash in French without knowing whether they should immediately translate it or not.

Even before the next morning's controls he knew that France-Dépêches would not show up well against the competition, having been behind with the news. Generally speaking, the agency that got used by a newspaper client was the one that delivered the story first. Among the English-language news-wires, competition was especially fierce.

With the last story of the day written and sent, for better or for worse, and after saying goodnight to Henri who went home to wife and child in Langata, Andy headed as usual for the Rainbow Bar in the city centre, bent on consolation.

As he ordered his first *Tusker baridi* (cold Tusker beer), a young woman leaned toward him from her bar-stool, put a hand on his arm, and asked him in a squeaky little voice to buy one for her too, which he did.

Njoki, for that was her name, was a keen conversationalist, and thirsty too. Several *Tusker baridi* later, she persuaded Andy to take her to the Starlite discotheque a few streets away, where they shimmied and shook to old records by Madonna, Whitney Houston and Tina Turner for an hour or two.

The young lady agreed thereafter to accompany him home for the night and enjoyed the ride to Westlands in Andy's battered old British open-top sports car, imported to Kenya at least twenty years earlier. He had recently bought it from another expatriate bachelor.

Like many fancy-free expats in Kenya and elsewhere in Africa, Andy took full and frequent advantage of the plentiful availability of young black women willing to have sexual intercourse with a *mzungu* (white man) in exchange for a few beers and a few banknotes in hard western currency.

For Andy, as for many others in Nairobi, be they *wazungu* (white men) or bar-girls, the foregoing encounter and exchange was a typical course of events – typical indeed of most of the hotels and bars of East and Central Africa. The AIDS scare of the late '80s and the '90s had receded and it was back to business as usual.

* * *

The next morning, Andy's grey-headed houseboy knocked on the bedroom door.

"Bleckfast for lady-friend?" he asked of the young master with a malevolent leer. Or was that a sneer?

"Yes please, Odwori," Andy replied wearily, emerging from a habitual Tusker beer hangover.

Odwori, a Luo from the shores of Lake Victoria in western Kenya, considered the young women of all Kenyan tribes apart from his own to be prostitutes. Njoki was a Kikuyu from Nyeri in Central Province, which includes the region around Nairobi.

Luos like Odwori also regarded the Kikuyu as the most mercenary tribe of all, second only to the *wahindi* (Asian Indians).

* * *

The same night, in a dreary but apparently desirable western suburb of Paris, Gareth Galant abruptly quit the home he shared with his wife Agathe. In point of fact, she virtually threw him out, though he was not sorry to leave.

"I know you've got another woman, and I even know who it is, so let's not discuss it any further. Just clear out of here and go to her, because that's what you want," she told him.

After eleven years of married life, their relationship was indeed at an end. Relations between them had been tense, glacial even, for months. Now Galant felt a sense of relief that things had finally come to a head after one of their frequent and apparently irrational quarrels.

They had for years been growing inexorably apart. Agathe, a former piano teacher and now the manageress of an esoteric book-store, came from a family of theosophists and classical musicians.

Her husband's materialist and Marxist view of the world, which he regarded as confirmed by the deepening world social and economic crisis, had long put him on a very different plane from hers.

Agathe resented the time and energy her husband devoted to political and trade union activities and was little interested in current affairs. He for his part found her individualistic and pessimistic view of human society insufferably depressing.

They had no children, for which Galant was now profoundly grateful.

Grabbing his briefcase, stuffing a clean shirt and some socks and underwear into it, together with his toothbrush, he closed the door on his wife, and then chose to walk down the four flights of stairs, although their block of flats had a lift. Breathing deeply, he felt oddly light-headed.

As soon as he reached the street he telephoned Marie-Claude Schroedinger. Marie-Claude was surprised to hear from him, especially when he asked if he could come round to her place, as they usually only met up twice a week and they had spent the previous night together. But she told him, in her typically formal manner, that he was always welcome.

The Metro was stifling hot and ill-smelling during Galant's 25-minute ride to the other side of the city.

Marie-Claude at first thought he had wanted to speak about trade union matters, and in particular the crisis at France-Dépêches, as the next day the unions were due to meet again with the managing director to discuss his 'action plan' for the agency, and she knew that a showdown was coming.

Right from the start of their relationship, Marie-Claude had made clear to Galant that she did not want to share him with his lawful wife. She wanted him to quit Agathe and for them to set up home together, although she had been careful never to insist or nag. Now it looked like what she had hoped for might happen.

He had already briefly told Marie-Claude on the phone that he was quitting his wife for her.

"Will Agathe give you a divorce?" she asked her lover, who had not yet really reflected on the question, soon after he entered her cosy little studio flat.

What Galant still did not know, because Marie-Claude had not thought it opportune to raise the question, was that she longed ardently to have a child by him. Now in her late thirties, Marie-Claude had begun to fear that motherhood would pass her by.

Even now, she dared not voice her desire, going only so far as to say that they would have to find a bigger apartment if they were to live together, another question which Galant had not yet really considered.

Emotionally, Marie-Claude was painfully repressed. Galant attributed this to the fact of her being the only child of old-fashioned and highly religious parents.

He had sensed her desperate need for love long before their physical relations began. It had disturbed and terrified him for many months during their trade union and party cell meetings before he finally yielded himself to her.

Even now, he would sometimes resist her love, fearing he might somehow drown in it, and retreated into a vague, moody silence. And this in turn terrified her.

As we all know, in such situations little things can mean so much. Thus when he now gently picked up her white angora cat, Pitchoune, placed it on his knees and stroked the animal, Marie-Claude read this as a positive omen.

Until now, he had always appeared indifferent toward the cat, ignoring it completely. Absurd though she knew this was, Marie-Claude saw Galant's unexpected and gentle gesture as a sign of her lover's paternal potential.

* * *

Delegates from the four unions met with the managing director in his penthouse office on the sixth floor of the France-Dépêches building in the Place de l'Horloge at their request at 1000 hours the next day, a Tuesday.

Like the first encounter of the previous week, this was not a happy one. The boss offered nothing new which merited a change in the unions' stance.

"My door is always open to any one or all of you for further detailed consultations," Juliet told them as he saw them out at the end of the fruitless session.

That sounded to Galant's ear like a veiled invitation to any union so inclined to break their so-far united ranks and deal unilaterally with him. The nuance was probably not lost on Ventrex either.

Whether the representatives of the other two unions had heard the implicit invitation was not clear. But what they lacked in intelligence they made up for in natural duplicity. Juliet's hint was perhaps unnecessary, for some of them were indeed already considering cutting a minority deal.

On the face of it, however, the *intersyndicale* – a sort of standing committee of the four unions – remained united and wholly opposed to Juliet's 'action plan'. Indeed, given that he had hardly varied at all in his position as outlined at their first meeting, they could scarcely do otherwise and still keep face.

The only positive element he had been able to offer was to promise that those staff whose jobs would disappear would be given priority for the new jobs created. But he still declined to indicate any numbers for the latter, while maintaining the expected number of job losses. A further union-management meeting was fixed for midday the following Thursday.

Galant then pressed Ventrex to agree that they should call another mass-meeting, for 1400 hours on the coming Friday, to report back to the staff of the outcome of their talks.

Ventrex was hesitant at first, saying that it was not yet clear what Juliet's final position was, but eventually agreed after Galant said they must keep everyone informed at every stage. Galant then told the other unions that the General Union and the Democratic Union had decided a new mass meeting was needed, to which they agreed.

* * *

The outbreak of suppurating fever was wreaking deadly havoc on the East Africa-Indian Ocean seaboard. As the disease spread to Madagascar, Mauritius, the Seychelles and all the major East African ports, most notably Mombasa, Dar Es Salaam and Durban, public panic mounted in inverse proportion to available facts and figures about the 'mystery disease'.

Eyewitness accounts spoke of harrowing scenes as

increasing numbers of poor, helpless people saw their nearest and dearest fall ill and die.

The World Health Organization contented itself with a figure of "probably some thousands" dead from the disease. Not only did the governments of the affected states prefer to downplay the matter; such was the imprecision of their data and their general anarchy that no-one had a clear idea of the numbers.

What one could say was that the plague was now spreading rapidly inland from the major seaports of Kenya, Tanzania, Mozambique and South Africa, erupting with particular virulence in the teeming insanitary townships around Nairobi and Johannesburg. There, public panic expressed itself in a violent hostility toward travellers or strangers considered potential carriers.

The Nairobi newspapers carried a particularly lurid account of the stoning to death of three Somali truck drivers. They had just arrived from Mombasa bound for Uganda with a load of rice and sugar and were seeking cheap lodgings for the night in the notorious township of Kalisha when they were set upon by a mob.

After the lapidation, their bleeding and battered bodies were doused with kerosene, set alight and abandoned in the street. The rice and sugar from their trucks was looted, and the trucks were driven away, no doubt soon to have their number plates changed.

The Mumbai, Singapore and Johannesburg stock exchanges all meanwhile fell in apparent connection with the epidemic.

At the same time, strangely, the disease seemed to have practically burned itself out on the Omarou islands, the supposed source of the outbreak, if the official local government figures reported by the France-Dépêches correspondent in Murumi, Omar Ali Sinbadi, could be believed. No new cases at all had been reported on Oreli, the 'breakaway' island, for several days.

According to popular rumour in Murumi, the disease had struck the people of Oreli as the result of a government curse in retaliation for their unilateral declaration of independence. Equally incredibly, the respite of the disease on Oreli was now locally attributed to an undertaking by the elders of the island to reconsider their position.

As to the nature of the disease, the WHO in Geneva said it had determined that it was chiefly borne by contaminated drinking water, but that infection could also spread from person to person by touch and did not rule out infection by the bite of mosquitoes breeding in contaminated water. People were advised to use only boiled water, to wash their hands frequently, and to avoid unnecessary contact with others such as shaking hands.

The WHO said it was hoping to develop a possible vaccine but stressed that at this stage these simple preventive measures offered the best protection.

The main coastal cities of Mombasa, Dar Es Salaam and Durban, along with a number of lesser port towns on the East African coast, had theoretically all been put under quarantine on the advice of the WHO. But inadequate, incompetent and corrupt local authorities, and the imperatives of continued transport and commerce, meant that anyone with a modicum of ingenuity or bribe money could enter or leave the towns at will, and so the disease continued to spread westward across the African continent.

CHAPTER 6

The habitual torpor of the agency's head offices in the Place de l'Horloge had in the course of ten days gradually given way to a pervading sense of bitterness, anger, shock and frustration among the staff. On the Friday morning before the second mass meeting, scheduled as before for 1400 hours, the tension in the production services, on the news desks and in the administrative and ancillary offices was almost palpable.

The crisis was exacerbating the personal animosities and political rivalries which characterise a complex and bureaucratic organisation such as this one, and not only among those with clear trade union or political affiliations; tempers were notably short and *bonhomie* in short supply; pessimism and cynicism were rife.

Many staff members simply feared for their livelihood and, in the view of a growing number, the very future of the agency itself appeared to be at stake in the struggle which was beginning to take shape.

Rumours of a union-management stalemate and impending confrontation appeared to be confirmed. *Libération* and *Le Monde* both carried articles that day foreseeing a 'critical showdown' at France-Dépêches. Again, evidently based on the same sources, both papers' reports emphasised the government's support for the managing director's 'action plan', which was, the articles' anonymous sources noted, in line with a general public policy of privatisation and a phasing-out of government subsidies wherever possible.

The new mass meeting, which this time began promptly, almost exactly on the appointed hour, took a similar form to that of a week earlier, with very much the same speakers dominating the debate. But the mood was much grimmer.

Galant spoke first, and he kept it short and to the point, dispensing with all rhetoric.

"Given the complete lack of positive response by Juliet to the unions' objections to his plan, your Democratic Union delegates see no alternative to a position of total refusal and resistance on the part of the personnel of France-Dépêches."

Ventrex opted for a dramatic note.

"Managing Director Christophe Juliet has, by his inflexible attitude, in effect indicated to the unions and the agency's staff as a whole that there is no room for any views apart from his own. The new boss of France-Dépêches has refused to negotiate," Ventrex pronounced.

"As Mr Juliet seems not to understand the nature of management-union relations, he may be forced to learn the hard way," Ventrex added. He had a tendency to bluster.

The assembly quickly grasped that the Galant-Ventrex tandem which dominated the *intersyndicale* was preparing the personnel for a trial of strength.

"Can you please tell us if the unions are already considering strike action?" requested one especially anxious German lady, as a gust of panic appeared simultaneously to afflict a number of persons of politically moderate disposition attending the mass meeting.

"How is it that we are already speaking of strike action? Is this not premature?" a spotty young man called out from the back of the large central newsroom before hunkering back down over his computer screen and keyboard.

Possibly encouraged by these signs of nervous disquiet, spokesmen for the two minority unions revealed that they hoped to negotiate further with Juliet, in particular on the number of job creations reserved for those who might lose their present posts.

Galant intervened again to say they could not rule out strike action, given the managing director's attitude and the issues at stake, while insisting that the unions hoped it would not come to that. He also stressed that there was no question of calling a strike without a ballot of the personnel.

Ventrex also chimed back in.

"We cannot rule out a strike, if that is the only language

the managing director understands," he declared, his voice rising to a near roar.

There was renewed debate about the government position.

For Ventrex it was clear: "Mr Juliet has the backing of his friend the finance minister." One could almost hear the curl of his lip as he spoke the words; the head of the agency's home news service could be an adroit demagogue when the occasion demanded.

Galant said they should not forget that in addition to the jobs at stake, there was the question of the agency's charter, its independence – "and therefore the very existence of France-Dépêches as we know it."

The mass meeting ended with a double decision: for the unions to go back to see the managing director for a final negotiating session, and for a delegation of the *intersyndicale* to urgently request an audience with the leaders of the main parliamentary political parties and the prime minister's office.

Unfortunately, such was the febrility and distraction of the occasion that a cardinal collective sin was committed that Friday afternoon. The Geneva bureau, whose staff was intently following the mass meeting over the radio-telephone link, managed to neglect for nearly an hour an urgent news communiqué from the World Health Organization.

The WHO announced that it had, in conjunction with a consortium of international pharmaceutical companies, "developed and tested in record time" a vaccine against the suppurating fever whose epidemic now held nearly half the African continent in its deadly thrall. Production of a first ten million doses of the vaccine had already begun and would be available for mass inoculation in the affected region within seven days.

This was major news, and yet, because of its internal crisis, the agency had been beaten hollow on the announcement by Amalgamated Press and Beckers, which both carried the news simultaneously from Geneva and UN headquarters in New York.

The WHO followed up its communiqué with a further important announcement a few hours later. This said that further talks had been held with other pharmaceutical companies, as a result of which the vaccine production consortium had been expanded and was preparing to produce twenty-five million doses, available within a month. Priority would be given to poor people living in bad conditions in shanty towns, the communiqué said.

This second announcement, which all the main news agencies reported rapidly, boosted pharmaceutical company shares significantly in Frankfurt, London and New York.

The WHO at the same time further revealed that it had asked "selected UN governments" to provide "teams of military medical corps" to administer the planned vaccination programme in eastern and southern Africa.

This extraordinary development – giving soldiers responsibility for medical care outside of a war situation – was appropriately given due prominence by France-Dépêches via its now fully-alerted New York bureau, as well as by the other main agencies.

Meanwhile local African media, quoting aid agency personnel, reported the first suspected cases of 'suppurating fever' in the Great Lakes and Nile source region of central Africa. The mortal disease was still spreading westward.

CHAPTER 7

At the agency's daily editorial conference on the Saturday morning, the normally mild-mannered deputy director of news was in a state of rage at the Geneva bureau's failure to report the WHO's 'suppurating fever' vaccine announcement in good time the previous day.

Determined that France-Dépêches get fully back on top of the story, he proposed the despatch of a special correspondent to the affected region, and asked the heads of the World news desk, the Africa news desk and the English-language desk who might be suitable.

As soon as the English desk head suggested a certain Cheryl Keyes, the deputy director of news decided she fitted the bill, thereby curtailing any misgivings or suggestions from other service chiefs. For Cheryl, although a French-Canadian from Montreal and therefore competent in French, wrote her news copy in English.

Sounded out by a telephone call, Cheryl responded that she was ready and willing to fly out immediately. Although it was her day off, she arrived back at the France-Dépêches headquarters by midday with passport and packed suitcase, but was then told that no flight was available until late Monday.

Cheryl, twenty-nine years old, a plump but pretty blonde, was full of energy and enthusiasm. Her mother was a French-Canadian former hospital nursing sister. Her father was a Scots-Canadian economist who had worked in Asia and Africa for the United Nations Conference on Trade and Development (UNCTAD) before settling his family in Quebec.

Recruited to France-Dépêches through the Ottawa bureau after a successful few years as local correspondent for a number of different media, Cheryl had been with the English service in Paris just over a year. She had covered a few diplomatic events when not sub-editing and translating for the agency. This was to be her first major assignment.

* * *

The morning of the following Monday, the trade union representatives met anew with the managing director as scheduled for a last-chance bid to head off the looming confrontation.

At this negotiating session, which began at 0930 hours and lasted till nearly 1300 hours with just a short break, Galant and Ventrex said little or nothing, leaving it to Juliet and the representatives of the two minority unions to try to find a compromise which would avoid an open union-management rupture while saving faces all round.

Despite the best efforts of the minority delegates, and some fastidious examination of details of the 'action plan', the managing director came up with nothing to get them off the hook.

But he did promise that he would, during the lunch-break, try to find out just how many new posts would be created as part of his 'action plan', thereby partly compensating for the expected job losses. He invited the unions to meet with him again at 1400 hours in his sixth-floor office.

On his return after lunch to his penthouse office on the top floor of the agency's headquarters, where he kept the delegation waiting some twenty minutes beyond the time he had fixed, Juliet was brisk and breezy in his response.

"Well, gentlemen. Having discussed your concerns with the development director and the finance director, I am able to say that we expect the new Internet and video services to provide between fifteen and twenty posts in all, about half-in-half for journalists and for information technicians. And like I said, the priority for these posts will, naturally, go to those whose jobs will disappear under the prior necessary restructuring of the agency."

Galant spoke for the first time that day.

"Is that really all you can offer in exchange for the loss of some seven hundred jobs?" he asked incredulously, voicing the thoughts of the entire union delegation.

The managing director sought to adopt a gentle conciliatory tone, but his attempt foundered upon on the rock of financial logic that had created the situation.

"Of course, it is a hard choice, but it's a necessary one.

Given that we must drastically reduce labour costs if we want to compete in the national and international media market, there would obviously be no point in creating as many jobs in new areas as we are forced to shed in others."

Ventrex too then spoke for the first time that day, to ask whether the management was really determined to press ahead with the planned change in the agency's charter. It was a rhetorical question, a change in the charter being a necessary condition for any kind of privatisation or 'opening up of the agency's capital', as the new government-inspired management language put it.

Turning toward Galant for the latter's tacit support and approval, and without waiting for a reply from Juliet, Ventrex delivered a warning shot with appropriate solemnity.

"Mr Juliet, the agency's trade unions are not prepared to stand by and watch the destruction of more than fifty years of independence at France-Dépêches. If necessary we will," Ventrex said, "take the battle into the political arena." Ventrex was no doubt thinking of his contacts with leaders of the opposition Socialist Party.

Juliet riposted that the question of the charter and future structure of the agency was indeed political, given that it was for the government and parliament to decide.

"So far as I understand it," he added, "the trade unions have no more than a consultative role in the matter, and I cannot help you there any further, gentlemen. But you are of course free to address your concerns in the appropriate quarter."

The suddenly provocative tone aside, Juliet was telling the unions that he had nothing more to offer, and that they should indeed therefore turn their attentions to the government and the political parties.

After these exchanges, the meeting appeared to grind to a natural halt. On behalf of all the delegates present, and with cold irony, Galant thanked the managing director for having received them and said the unions would be reporting back to their members on the outcome of the talks.

As they quit the sixth floor, Galant informed Ventrex in an aside that he would be calling an emergency meeting of all sections of the Democratic Union and that he expected the question of strike action to be debated.

"I don't see that we have much alternative," was all that Ventrex responded.

Galant realised then that for all his bluster, his long-time trade union rival had no real stomach for the fight. He also detected a strong smell of alcohol on his colleague's breath, which was consistent with a slightly glassy-eyed look.

Meanwhile, after an extended Indian summer, the

weather in Paris, in this third week of October, had suddenly turned markedly cold.

* * *

Late that evening, discussing the situation at the agency while lying in bed alongside Marie-Claude in her little Paris apartment, Galant expressed his fear and suspicion that the minority unions secretly supported the proposed change in the charter, if not the privatisation plan too.

"Are they naïve, or what?" asked Marie-Claude.

"What difference does it make whether they are sincere, naïve or whatever?" he snapped back, for once blind to the breathtakingly beautiful form beside him.

"Ideologically, objectively, whatever you want, that's the way they are, and it's damned dangerous. They are in favour of private investment and they are prepared to undo the agency charter to achieve that!"

Galant was tense and tired. She consoled him by gently sliding a slim pale thigh across his hips and nuzzling his neck and chest, and thus they spoke no more of agency or political matters that night.

* * *

At Paris's Orly airport, Cheryl Keyes boarded an Air France flight to Nairobi via Kigali and Bujumbura. It would be her first time in Africa, and she was apprehensive, as well as excited.

For her, air travel remained a novel experience. As the big passenger jet accelerated to the end of the runway and began its shuddering sharp lift into the air, she suffered a moment of panic in the pit of her stomach, followed by a ripple of nervous pleasure the length of her thighs and down the spine. Her thoughts and sensations made her feel strangely childlike and vulnerable.

Earlier that evening, on the way to Orly, Cheryl had had to deal with a Tunisian taxi-driver evidently deeply impressed by her blond curls and curvaceous figure. He eagerly practiced his rudimentary English on her.

"You have husband? You have children?"

Cheryl was uncomfortably aware of his glittering dark eyes scrutinising her in the rear-view mirror.

She managed not to be rude to the taxi-driver, while still telling him in formal French to mind his own business and to keep his eyes on the road.

Proud that she had been able to fend him off verbally, Cheryl briefly pondered asking him a question about the recent revolution in his country, but thought better of it, for fear of saying something possibly unwise. *That was a useful precaution for the future,* she thought.

"You're not on duty right now," she told herself, only to

realise with a strange sense of premonition that she would likely soon be crossing that line between on- and off-duty.

Among the recreational reading matter she had taken with her on the recommendation of an amusing and sympathetic male colleague was a copy of Joseph Conrad's *A Heart of Darkness*.

CHAPTER 8

Gareth Galant, Marie-Claude Schroedinger and a growing number of other staff members at France-Dépêches were beginning to feel the weight of the struggle into which they had entered and sought to analyse it.

The situation seemed clear enough. Having recently gained direct representation in government, and having already attacked a number of public services on behalf of private enterprise, ascendant right-wing capitalist forces now had their eyes on what they saw as the lucrative potential of France-Dépêches. These forces wanted to milk the agency for whatever its assets and earning powers were worth financially.

"People like Juliet, this government, care nothing for editorial independence or people's jobs. They are just out to loot the agency."

That was what Galant told a meeting of the agency's Democratic Union sections, hastily convened for a vote on the question of strike action if Juliet did not withdraw his plan.

To his satisfaction, the DU journalists and employees voted overwhelmingly in favour of a strike if the 'action plan' was not withdrawn unconditionally. The strike motion was carried by twenty-nine votes with three abstentions and none against.

Galant immediately informed Ventrex of the decision, confident now that the latter's numerically more powerful and influential General Union would be bound to follow suit.

The fact remained, however, that many if not most members of staff were still undecided; for them, the situation, the alternatives, were still not clear.

Those of a right-wing or conservative bent argued that France-Dépêches needed exposure to market forces, and should no longer rely on French government financial support, which they said was bad for its image of supposed editorial independence and provided a sinecure for the lazy and incompetent.

Those more on the left argued that the agency's editorial independence would be compromised by any privatisation, and that jobs and conditions must be defended at all costs.

A battle for hearts and minds, with the main stakes being the future of the French news agency France-Dépêches, was in effect now under way.

* * *

The fortnightly meeting of the local cell of Workers Power, held in the upper room of a shabby *bistrot* near the Place de l'Horloge and once frequented by print-workers, was largely devoted to the situation at France-Dépêches.

But the meeting first heard a report from Marie-Claude Schroedinger on the general political situation in the country and the immediate tasks of Workers Power comrades.

In sum, she said that with the multiplication of different struggles by sectors such as the public service workers and the teachers, the situation was tending objectively towards one of a general strike against the government.

However, for reasons of bureaucratic self-interest, the national leaders of the General Union and the Democratic Union were continually dividing the ranks of the working class, rather than seeking to unify them against the government.

"The task of Workers Power is therefore to expose these divisive tactics – not by simply denouncing the leaders responsible for them – but by tirelessly proposing practical united action. Such action is difficult for the bureaucrats to reject openly."

It was a classic analysis and response to a classic situation, and perfectly correct in so far as it went. But Marie-Claude, for all her devotion, and notwithstanding her impressive physical beauty, was as usual cold and unconvincing in her speech. Her monotone wooden delivery, on the basis of prepared notes, gave the unfortunate impression that she was simply repeating by rote what she had been told to say.

In fact, she was terribly self-conscious, by nature tense and strictly self-controlled. Marie-Claude totally lacked the self-confidence, the political instincts and powers of analysis that Gareth Galant displayed, and which nourished her fiercely burning love for him.

In his report, Galant informed cell comrades that the agency was possibly heading for a first-ever strike by all the personnel if the government's job-cuts and privatisation plan was not rapidly withdrawn.

"There is one clear, obvious obstacle to the government's plan, and that is the strength of organisation of the agency's personnel as represented by the trade unions, or at least the perception of that strength," he stated with emphasis.

"Whatever the objective truth of the matter, France-Dépêches is apparently considered a bastion of trade union power in the French media, judging by recent reports on the crisis in these same media. We in the DU are thus a key factor.

"All I can say," he added after a pause, "is that the Democratic Union position, firmly based on the interests of the staff and the general public interest as a whole, has been gaining ground and is winnable.

"Any defence against Juliet and his 'action plan' can only be based upon the consciousness of the staff, not only of their immediate material interests, but also of the need to defend the agency. And given the seriousness of the threat, that defence can only be based on a call for strike action."

Galant paused again before continuing.

"However, we still need time to convince many staff members, particularly those in the provinces or abroad. The key to the success of this struggle will be to maintain unity within the *intersyndicale* and among the staff as a whole on a clear and simple line."

Galant again spelled out the simple line to which he hoped the unions would adhere: "The managing director must withdraw his unacceptable plan before there can be any further talks of any kind, or else face strike action."

DU headquarters had been kept informed of the crisis and had promised its support "whatever that's worth", Galant remarked offhandedly, only to add: "We should have no illusions. It will be largely up to our leadership, here on the ground, whether the personnel, journalists and other employees, win this struggle or not."

At least one of the minority unions supported the idea of a change in the agency's status to open it up for private investment and was thus "offering its services" to the management and the government, Galant told his party comrades. Quite how he knew this was not clear, but it seemed more than likely.

However, until now, none of the other unions had so

far dared openly break ranks, Galant noted. Crucially, the General Union sections were so far holding firm. "Our strategy must be to force them to maintain unity," he stressed, warning that divisive tactics were to be feared and expected at this stage.

"Most important for us is that the Stalinists in the General Union are today much weaker than they were before the Berlin Wall fell and the USSR collapsed, and so they are therefore less able by their tactics to frustrate the will of the workforce."

At the close of the cell meeting, Marie-Claude was mandated to write an article on the crisis at the agency for the Workers Power weekly newspaper. The short unsigned article, which appeared in the party paper the following week, and which was in fact heavily rewritten by Galant, gave no hint of his fears.

Stressing the united front presented by the General Union, the Democratic Union and the others, it noted that previous plans of this sort for the agency had all failed.

But the article also drew a parallel with a successful government plan more than twenty-five years earlier to break up and part-privatise the French state broadcasting corporation, while noting that the political situation was today rather different, notably due to a weakened official Communist Party.

CHAPTER 9

Bertrand Rainier, chief of the France-Dépêches bureau in Nairobi, which was responsible for the agency's news coverage of the East African and Indian Ocean region, was an odious, ill-tempered man, though often managed to hide this under a thick layer of smarmy hypocrisy.

He had only been back at work in the Kenyan capital for three days after his Paris trip when he was informed by a Saturday morning telephone call from the deputy director of news that Paris was sending a special correspondent to the region to help cover the epidemic of suppurating fever.

That in itself was enough to annoy and worry Rainier, for any France-Dépêches journalist sent to work on his patch as a special correspondent he regarded as a potential threat to his authority. That Cheryl Keyes was both an anglophone writer and a woman only augmented his displeasure.

Rainier would not admit to such 'anti-anglo' or misogynist feelings, any more than he would admit to his openly racist attitudes, which he illustrated with jokes in bad taste and contemptuous treatment of the local black staff of the Nairobi bureau and his long-suffering houseboy.

By no means stupid, however, he was aware that Paris had become critical of the coverage of the viral plague story by the regional bureau, and he felt guilty about his absence during an important running story, having delayed his return from France for reasons still unrevealed.

As head of the agency's regional bureau, it was incumbent on Rainier to welcome Cheryl when her plane landed at Jomo Kenyatta airport. So there he was early that morning, forcing a fake smile and asking her in imperfect heavily accented English if she had had a good flight.

She noted his reluctance to shake hands, as well as his greasy, over-long hair and got a strong whiff of the sickly-smelling aftershave or cologne that he used.

Rainier took Cheryl to the hotel where a room had been booked for her. The Nairobi bureau had put her in a new place called The Excalibur.

"How ridiculous," Cheryl said to herself on learning the name of the hotel. *Who round here would know the origin of that name?* she thought rather uncharitably. Cheryl had read her elder brother's copy of the tales of King Arthur and his Knights of the Round Table at the age of twelve.

The bureau chief left her at the hotel around nine that morning to freshen up and overcome any jet-lag as best as possible after the eight-hour night flight and invited her to come to the office at midday "to discuss the work you will be doing".

After a fitful doze, Cheryl duly presented herself at the regional bureau offices, where she was warmly greeted by

Andy Mitchell and Henri Laborie before knocking on the chief's door.

"*Entrez*," Rainier intoned and waved her toward a corner seat in his spacious office. He was sat behind a huge almost bare desk.

Looking over a pair of half-spectacles intended to convey the seriousness of his purpose, the bureau chief now opted to speak French to the newly-arrived special correspondent. No doubt so that what he had to say would be perfectly understood. And no doubt realising that his English was inadequate for the task.

"It's best I remind you now that you are working for the French news agency, not for the English desk or the English service. Your copy must be read by me before being sent to Paris, or if I am not present, either by Andy or Henri. Is that clear?"

Cheryl already knew of Rainier's bad reputation but was nevertheless stunned to receive such a complete confirmation of it so soon. What he had just said went without saying, so why say it? She knew the rules. *What an asshole!* she thought.

She nodded and was about to voice a meek word of acknowledgement, but the bureau chief ploughed on without a pause.

"You should also realise that the cost of your

assignment – apart from the airfare from Paris and back – comes out of the Nairobi bureau budget. That means that your expenses while you are in the region have to be approved by me."

Cheryl decided this was not the moment to tell him she had been provided with some funds in dollars by the agency before leaving Paris, thanks to the foresight of the deputy director of news, with whom she had a brief but friendly talk before heading for the airport.

Like a certain number of middle-management figures in France-Dépêches, Rainier alternately feared, hated and envied the agency's English-language journalists and the English-language news desk, imagining them to be somehow more dynamic or professional than their French counterparts. On top of which he was by nature suspicious of his colleagues and generally paranoid.

Notwithstanding her foreknowledge of Rainier's reputation, Cheryl in her naivety had imagined that the bureau chief's first subject of conversation with her would be about the coverage of the epidemic of viral plague fever which was devastating the region. In point of fact he barely touched upon the work she was to do.

He surprised her, however, with a sudden attempt at light conversation at the end of the interview, when he gestured toward the picture window. "We're privileged up here," he said. She wondered what he was trying to say.

How did being on the top and thirteenth floor of a central Nairobi skyscraper count as a privilege? she wondered, but did not have to wait long for the explanation.

"On a clear day like today you can see the snows of Kilimanjaro. Can you see it?" the boss asked.

Cheryl was short-sighted, and because she had been a bit bleary-eyed after the night flight had not put her contact lenses in. But by screwing up her eyes, she thought she could just make out the white peak on the horizon, evidently a good many miles to the south.

Taking her leave of the man, Cheryl vaguely wondered about Rainier's position in relation to the current crisis within the agency. Andy Mitchell and Henri Laborie could have explained to her that he was such a sycophant that he really had no position at all of his own.

"Trust him to side with the top management, save in the event that the trade unions are successful in their opposition," Andy would have said.

If ever a man wanted to be on the winning side, that was Rainier. There were a number of others like him in this respect in the agency, as no doubt there are in other comparable organisations.

* * *

In the agency's Place de l'Horloge headquarters in Paris,

Gareth Galant informed Ventrex that the Democratic Union membership had voted in favour of holding a secret ballot of all staff members of the agency for a renewable 24-hour strike if Juliet did not withdraw his 'action plan'. He would, he told his rival, be arguing for such a course of action at the next mass meeting, which was scheduled for the coming Friday at the usual time of 1400 hours.

Ventrex for his part informed Galant that meetings had been requested with the leaders of all the main political parties represented in parliament for the middle of the following week, and that the prime minister's office had promised to reply to a request made by the *intersyndicale* for an audience.

He added that the General Union members would also be meeting before Friday and that he expected the GU to support a strike call if the managing director did not back down.

The two men briefly debated whether they wanted representatives of all four unions to meet in a further session of the *intersyndicale* ahead of Friday's mass meeting, before agreeing that they should not offer the minority unions the chance to divide the movement at this point. Both men sensed a definite gain of momentum in their favour and wanted nothing to run counter to that.

When the third mass meeting in as many weeks came round, both Galant for the Democratic Union and Ventrex for the General Union arrived armed with a clear mandate on behalf of their respective members to propose a strike ballot.

The turn-out at the meeting was the highest yet; the main editorial room on the third floor of the agency building was packed, with people sitting on desks if they could not find a chair, and people were standing in all the aisles between the desks.

Amid a sudden hush, Galant turned to his rival and addressed him in an undertone.

"Paul, we will explain the gravity of the situation to the staff, and the absolute need for a united front, because we need a vote in favour of a strike, OK? We must demand that Juliet withdraw his plan unconditionally before there can be any further talks, OK?"

Ventrex could only agree.

Galant proposed that he himself give an account of events up to this point, and that Ventrex propose the strike ballot. To this Ventrex could not help but agree too. He well understood that Galant wanted to fully implicate him in joint leadership of the battle ahead.

Testifying to the evolution of the situation over the last fortnight or so, the debate at this mass meeting moved beyond the details and implications of the managing director's 'action plan', concentrating rather on the exact question that was to be posed in the strike ballot.

The minority unions, for the meanwhile at least, appeared to have swung round to a position of full support for the proposed strike call.

After a brief consultation with colleagues from the other unions, Ventrex put to the mass meeting the following resolution:

"Given the need to defend the jobs of salaried personnel and to preserve the independence of France-Dépêches, this general assembly of agency staff calls on Managing Director Christophe Juliet to withdraw his unacceptable 'action plan', failing which the intersyndicale will organise a ballot for a 24-hour renewable strike in all bureaux and services beginning 15 November."

The resolution was overwhelmingly carried, with 331 votes in favour, seventy-five against and forty-three abstentions. Galant, Ventrex and two other union representatives immediately took the lift to the sixth floor to inform Juliet of the resolution that had been voted and to hand him a copy. They requested a response from him within forty-eight hours.

CHAPTER 10

Jean-François Cardenal, director of the important France-Dépêches regional bureau in Santa de Costa, was barely out of bed and expecting to follow his usual leisurely daily routine when, with unusual haste and clamour, the housemaid Maria banged on the bedroom door and called out shrilly: "*Señor, telefon !*"

Taking the call on the landing, Cardenal heard his deputy Pierre Grangier inform him that there had been a failed *coup d'état* attempt against the Santa de Costa government of President Felipe Lopez shortly before dawn that morning.

Loyal troops had been deployed and controlled the capital, but the situation was still very tense. Cardenal looked out the window of his luxury hilltop villa onto the palm-fringed boulevard below but saw nothing out-of-the-ordinary.

"How are we covered on the story?" he asked Grangier.

"Not too well, I'm afraid," his deputy replied. It emerged that the Spanish- and Portuguese-language wires had given the news promptly, and followed it up with detailed colour and background, but that the bureau's French journalists had been nearly an hour behind and so far had given just some bare facts based on the government radio station's report.

"Get them onto it now!" the bureau chief commanded superfluously.

Better late than never, his deputy had in fact already roused the bureau's French staff and the agency's roving regional anglophone correspondent, Peter Morel. Cardenal knew he should expect a chastising phone-call shortly from the director of news, and so hurried to the bureau offices where he made a rare show of serious professional purpose.

Again, the deep crisis within France-Dépêches had distracted the attention of a bureau's journalists, allowing the agency's competitors, Amalgamated News and Beckers, to take the lead on a story. But worse was to come, and for this too Jean-François Cardenal would be held at least partly responsible.

Until now, Cardenal had thoroughly enjoyed his position as chief of the France-Dépêches regional bureau in Santa de Costa City. An old-fashioned journalist of the kind still occasionally found in the higher echelons of the conservative French print media, he bore the stamp of Establishment birth and fortune. Elegant and urbane, he would more easily pass for a career diplomat than a wire-service journalist.

Thanks to the status of his post, as well as an advantageous marriage, Jean-François Cardenal figured high on the local cocktails- and dinner-party circuit. Ably seconded by his beautiful Santa de Costan wife Constanza, a former fashion model and the daughter of a prominent banker, he devoted considerable agency time and money to entertaining.

Of course, it was the task of the agency's regional bureau chief to keep a finger on the political pulse. It was appropriate and useful that diplomats and minor ministers dine at his table. But the price to be paid for such a profile was that, among the foreign press corps in Santa de Costa, Cardenal was regarded as an unofficial agent of the French foreign ministry, if not of the French secret services.

At the very least, it was presumed that the Quai d'Orsay had approved his posting. And perhaps indeed all this was not so far from the truth.

Cardenal's journalism rarely went beyond the occasional geopolitical 'analysis piece' based on the views of unnamed 'regional observers'. He entrusted his editorial lieutenants with the job of reporting the daily news, concentrating for his part on providing 'the big picture'. It was all the more ironical, therefore, that he should have been so surprised by the coup bid in Santa de Costa and its dramatic aftermath. But he was by no means alone in that.

According to commentators such as himself, the small Central American state of Santa de Costa was a beacon of democratic stability in a sub-continent permanently awash with revolutionary effervescence, *coups d'état* and military dictatorship. No doubt this was the reason that the top management of France-Dépêches had, some years earlier, decided to establish the agency's regional bureau, with responsibility for the news coverage of all Latin America and part of the Caribbean, in Santa de Costa City.

Now, in a peaceful general election a year ago, just before Cardenal was named to his post, the people of Santa de Costa had for the first time elected a majority of Social Democrat deputies, leading to the formation of a first centre-left government after years of unbroken Christian Democrat rule.

Right-wing conservatives warned of impending 'socialist measures', but the government of President Felipe Lopez had so far sought to appease the big landowners whose coffee and fruit plantations were the backbone of the country's economy. President Lopez had in fact maintained the liberal economic policies of his predecessors.

In the absence of a significant industrial working class, poor peasants and plantation workers had, along with a few self-important and increasingly discredited intellectuals, long formed the social base of the country's Socialist and Communist parties.

But in recent years an independent agrarian movement demanding radical land reform had also emerged, outside the control of the traditional left-wing parties, and this had been worrying the land- and plantation-owners, which explained their support for the coup attempt.

In the event, however, few military officers and men

rallied to the plotters' call to overthrow 'the socialist regime', and the coup bid quickly turned into a fiasco and fizzled out.

According to popular rumour, the four obsolete armoured cars which trained their cannons on the president's office and called on him to resign in favour of a putative 'Salvation Council' did not even have shells for their guns, while the men sent to take the government radio station apparently lacked the necessary resolve at the last moment.

But President Lopez was furious, indignantly accusing 'imperialist agents' of having fomented the attempted putsch. In the days immediately following the coup bid, the government ordered the expulsion of a number of US 'military advisors' on secondment to the country's armed forces and called on peasants and workers to demonstrate their support for President Lopez and their rejection of 'the fascist imperialist plotters'.

There was outrage among left-wing intellectuals in the Western world, some of whom even compared events in Santa de Costa to the US-backed coup against Salvador Allende's government in Chile in 1973.

President Lopez was possibly himself embarrassed by the effusive messages of support he now received from Hugo Chavez in Venezuela and Raul Castro in Cuba, among others. He had so far been trying to steer some kind of middle course.

But testifying to the strength of the long pent-up pressures that had brought the Lopez government to power a year earlier, and to the impatience that had been building up since, trade union and agrarian leaders responded with impressive vigour to the president's call to 'defend democracy'. Many of the fruit and coffee plantations were 'occupied' by their workers, amid calls for a 'true workers' and peasants' government' under trade union control and for redistribution of large foreign-owned plantations to landless peasants.

Within days of the abortive coup bid, the government found itself forced to concede to the *de facto* nationalisation of all large foreign-owned land holdings, in a move regarded by left-wing political theorists as the essential first step towards the peasant movement's long-sought goal of agricultural reform. In short, another revolutionary process was now under way in Latin America.

* * *

Representatives of the *intersyndicale* at France-Dépêches headquarters in Paris, having heard no further word from Juliet by the deadline of midday the following Monday, began organising the strike ballot. They determined that a total of 1891 eligible staff should be asked to cast a 'yes' or 'no' vote by secret ballot on the following question:

Given the need to defend jobs and to preserve the independence of France-Dépêches, do you agree with the trade unions' proposal for a 24-hour renewable strike beginning 15 November if the managing director does not withdraw his unacceptable 'action plan'?

Paris-based staff were invited to cast their votes in one of three ballot boxes which were established in the staff canteen. A service note sent by the *intersyndicale* to all provincial and foreign bureaux asked them each to organise a ballot and to transmit the result to Paris. The deadline for valid votes was fixed for midnight Sunday, 31 October.

CHAPTER 11

By this point, most of France-Dépêches was in a state of febrility. The epicentre of the fever was the agency's Place de l'Horloge headquarters, where the Paris news desks and production services were especially affected. From there it radiated outwards to the far corners of the agency's global news network.

The strike ballot, which was due to last the whole week, provoked renewed eruptions of nervous anxiety and angry incomprehension among agency staff near and far, as they were asked to hold meetings on the proposed rejection of the 'action plan' and then vote and transmit the result to the *intersyndicale* in Paris.

There was a great sense of uncertainty among the agency's staff at all levels about the course on which they were embarking, and this caused tensions to mount during the course of the week.

It was perhaps in the natural order of things that such a process should exacerbate social conflicts and divisions. But at the same time, the process prompted earnest and intelligent debate about the issues at stake. For many this was a novel situation. New affinities as well as new animosities were forged, new questions were in the air.

If the vote were positive and the strike went ahead as proposed on all the agency's news-wires, this would be the first time in the France-Dépêches history of more than sixty years that its services to clients had been completely halted by a strike. Most of those voting had never imagined that they might be involved in such an action.

* * *

The director of news was once again unhappy with the performance of the Santa de Costa regional bureau, which had not grasped the context and significance of the nationalisation of all large foreign-owned plantations, at least not until the US government had made its concerns known.

The State Department issued a clear and potentially threatening warning. "The United States government cannot accept the alienation and seizure of private property without due process and without guarantees of appropriate compensation," the statement from the Obama administration said.

This was the voice of Secretary of State Hillary Clinton speaking on behalf of US capitalist interests.

The director of news was in an especially bad mood following that morning's editorial conference in Paris, which Paul Ventrex attended in his capacity as head of the French domestic news service. Ventrex had thrown a violent tantrum, roundly criticising virtually all the agency's executive editors for incompetence.

Coverage of events in Latin America, Africa or Asia

was in no way the responsibility of Ventrex, of course. He was the head of the domestic – that is to say, strictly French – news-gathering and -disseminating operations, and no way in charge of foreign news. But this did not prevent him from minding other people's business.

The director of news had, not for the first time, received the definite impression that Ventrex, exploiting the general sense of crisis, was after his job and by his criticisms seeking to pave the way to obtaining it.

In his exasperation at the poor Santa de Costa coverage, the director of news ordered Cardenal to have his bureau translate an article on events in the country written by the regional anglophone correspondent, Peter Morel. For Morel, recently back from trips to Venezuela, Bolivia and Ecuador, and evidently inspired by his experience in those countries, had "put a sexy revolutionary spin" on the Santa de Costa story, in the words of the director of news.

"That's what you and your people should be writing too, that's what the world wants to know about, that's why Washington is so concerned, isn't it, Jean-François? Bloody revolution!" he barked down the phone before hanging up on the hapless Cardenal.

Cardenal thereupon confided the task of translating Morel's copy to Pierre Grangier. As was often the case in a large bureau such as this one, the second-in-command did much of the hard work when he did not organise that of others. It was ignominious to have to translate a more junior colleague's copy, and so Grangier was keen to get it over and done with quickly.

Privately, he too grumbled about his boss's incompetence. "Ignorant, aristocratic *dilettante!*" he fumed.

* * *

In Paris, a delegation of the *intersyndicale* had succeeded in meeting with representatives of the main political parties in the French National Assembly. An account of the exchanges was posted on all agency notice-boards Place de l'Horloge and sent out to all bureaux in the form of a special service note signed by delegates of the four unions.

The left-wing opposition parties had expressed their sympathy and understanding, and promised to express the unions' fears when it came to an examination in parliamentary committee of the proposed amendments to the agency charter. But they virtually admitted their impotence, in view of their minority situation.

Predictably, the government parties simply listened politely before indicating that they believed a part-privatisation of the agency and the phasing out of state subsidies for such an institution were both desirable and necessary. This was also in accordance with the mandate of the government which they were committed to support, they said in substance.

Interestingly, however, the union delegation learned

that the proposed amendment to the agency charter did not yet figure on the current legislative timetable. Checking with the prime minister's office, the *intersyndicale* also discovered that, contrary to expectations, the proposed bill was not scheduled to be considered by any government cabinet meeting "for the meanwhile".

The *intersyndicale* renewed its request for an audience with the prime minister.

* * *

Far from the Paris hothouse, Cheryl Keyes immersed herself in the 'suppurating fever' story, working happily together with Henri Laborie and Andy Mitchell who both joked along with her all day long. Confined to bed by a bout of malaria, Nairobi bureau chief Rainier was in no shape to bother them.

To get her out of the office, Cheryl took the narrow-gauge railway night-train to Mombasa for a rapid reportage on the ravages of the disease and the start of a vaccination campaign in the Indian Ocean port city, accompanied by agency photographer Jim Alexander, who had been seconded from the Johannesburg bureau for a few days. To collective satisfaction in Nairobi and Paris, their reportage and pictures 'scored' well in newspapers all round the world.

She even found time for two hours on a magnificent beach of white sand a few miles south of Mombasa, excitedly dipping her toes in the Indian Ocean and drinking the milk of a fresh coconut, accompanied by the bored and moody photographer from Jo'burg, who proved an unwilling chaperone. He was evidently unimpressed by this dizzy blonde on the loose in Africa. For reasons known only to himself, he wanted to get back home to Johannesburg as soon as possible.

On her return to Nairobi, Cheryl attended a further World Health Organization news conference in the UN offices at Gigiri, accompanied by Henri. This time they were well-organised and got the hard news out fast, with Andy in the office taking dictation alternately in English and in French, banging the copy into bite-sized shape and form and sending it promptly down the wires to the English and the French news desks in Paris for redistribution to agency clients round the world.

The news from the WHO was little short of sensational and announced simultaneously in Geneva and New York too. More military medical corps, provided by the US, the British, the Canadian and the French armed forces – an intended 550 persons or so in all – were to be deployed to administer the second batch of vaccine in and around Mombasa, Dar Es Salaam, Nairobi, Maputo, Durban, Johannesburg and Cape Town.

The France-Dépêches team in Nairobi was first to flash the news, ahead of the competition, before the Geneva and New York bureaux took over the story to handle the political and economic implications of the announcement.

Although the total number of vaccine doses expected to be produced and administered was still officially put at twenty-five million and no more for the meanwhile, pharmaceutical company shares rose significantly again on the world's stock exchanges.

While waiting for the WHO news conference to begin, Cheryl had time to notice among her journalist colleagues the presence of a tall handsome black man, casually but elegantly dressed in a mix of western and traditional African styles.

Accompanying Henri and Andy the following evening to a house party given by the doyen of Nairobi's Scandinavian press corps, Bengt Danielssen, in the upper-class district of Muthaiga, she saw the same man again, before their host introduced them to each other.

CHAPTER 12

You could not say that Cheryl Keyes had led a completely sheltered life till now, but she was not especially worldly-wise either; her liberal middle-class upbringing had protected her from the crueller realities of life.

Her formative years were spent in third-world countries to which her father was posted. She and her brother had attended schools in compounds and suburbs strictly for white expatriates. She had thus been shocked at the sight of dirty drunken *clochards* lying on the Paris pavements, and even more so by the crippled beggars on the streets of Nairobi.

At the age of twenty-nine, love and romance had not especially blossomed for Cheryl yet. In Ottawa she had been virtually engaged to a quantity surveyor for nearly five years, but had found herself bored and frustrated with the kindly but dull David. By the time she left Ottawa and him for the France-Dépêches job in Paris, their relationship had died a natural death.

Since then, she had had two or three brief romantic adventures of little interest or account. The pleasures of being single again, and in Paris with a stimulating job, had balanced the loneliness and lack of love.

Cheryl had shared an occasional whiff of marijuana in her college days and had learned since to appreciate good wines and was especially fond of *kir*. But her encounter with the tall black man at Bengt Danielssen's house party in Nairobi was like the rush of a dangerous drug.

As he took her hand, shook it firmly and held it just a little longer than was normal or necessary, searching her face before lowering his eyes to appraise her body, Cheryl felt a lurch somewhere in her lower organs and blushed deeply.

Otelo Okello was his name, though he invited acquaintances to call him Otto. Otto Okello was what Bengt Danielssen introduced him as. Otto, she learned much later, had asked Bengt to present him to "the pretty blonde journalist", and Bengt needed discreetly to ask Andy to repeat her name for himself first.

Otto, like many of the guests that night, was also a journalist. He was, he told her, a senior editor of the PanAfrican News Agency, or PANA, an organisation of which Cheryl had never heard. He was in East Africa to cover the viral plague story, he said.

"Bingo!" Cheryl blurted out nervously, then revealed to the handsome African that she was in the region on a similar assignment.

Otto asked her if she knew so-and-so from the France-Dépêches bureau in Dakar, Senegal – a good friend of his, he said – but as yet she knew few of the agency's journalists posted around the world. Otto congratulated Cheryl on her reportage in Mombasa, which he had seen and read "in the Western press", as he put it.

"Can I bring you a beer?"

Beer was not really Cheryl's drink, but Otto said it was the thing to drink in Africa, so she accepted. He brought her an opened, foaming bottle of Primus, and no glass.

"Imported from Congo," he informed her. "It's the best."

He drank his beer straight from the bottle and watched her with a smile as she followed suit.

"Cheryl, I'm going to visit the township of Karawangi to see what's happening with the fever and the vaccinations. I've heard that *askari wazungu* (white European soldiers, he explained) are wanting to give people injections there, and that the people are afraid and have been running away. Would you like to come with me?"

"When?"

"When you like. Perhaps tomorrow?"

"I don't know."

She needed time to think.

"Can I call you at your office?"

"OK."

"One thing. We can't go taking pictures, it's dangerous there, especially for a white woman. You don't speak any African language. I will have to speak Kiswahili for both of us..."

As Cheryl rather expected he would, Otelo Okello phoned her the very next morning, and she already knew that she would accept his offer, having talked to Andy and Henri about it on their way home from the party. They saw no problem. The bureau chief was still sick with malaria, while the photographer was already on his way back to Jo'burg.

Otto chose a very battered-looking taxi to take them to Karawangi. The township was much further out of the town centre than Cheryl had imagined. As the taxi bumped over the badly-kept dusty red murram road, Otto talked about himself. Cheryl knew that he wanted to impress her, but still enjoyed his seductive patter.

His mother was an Acholi from northern Uganda, his father a Dinka from southern Sudan. "These are Nilotic tribes, not like the Kikuyu or the Kamba of central Kenya, who are Bantu," he explained. "We are very black, and we are not circumcised."

When he was thirteen or fourteen he had been adopted by a wealthy Swahili trader who lived from the illicit cross-border commerce between northern Uganda, eastern Congo (or Zaire as it then was) and southern Sudan. In addition to his parents' tribal tongues, he spoke the vehicular Kiswahili and Lingala, as well as English and French.

"But I can only read and write in Kiswahili, English and French."

His first name, which Cheryl belatedly grasped was a form of Othello, as in the Shakespeare play of that name, had been bestowed upon him through the influence of some Italian nuns who ran a missionary hospital in the northern Ugandan town of Gulu, near his mother's home village.

At one point in the journey, their taxi was obliged to stop at a makeshift roadblock manned by three gun-toting paramilitary policemen. One of the policemen lowered his head to the car window and spoke to the driver. The driver then spoke to Otto who immediately extracted a banknote from his wallet and handed it to the driver who placed it into the policeman's discreetly waiting hand.

As they drove off again after being waved on by the policemen, Cheryl asked Otto what they had wanted.

"The policeman said they were thirsty and needed *chai*."

Otto and the taxi-driver both laughed at this *bon mot*. Only much later did Cheryl learn that *chai* was not only Kiswahili for 'tea' but could also mean a bribe in notoriously corrupt Kenya.

Try as they might, when they got to Karawangi and found their way to the dispensary where the vaccinations were being carried out – "voluntarily", the US medical orderly in charge who declined to give his name pointed out – they found no evidence of people having run away in fear of the injections. All was proceeding in complete calm, it seemed.

If he was disappointed that the rumour of forced vaccinations was not borne out, Otto did not show it. Cheryl later stitched together an adequate reportage. She never did find out what, if anything, Otto wrote. They were anyway both of them more interested in each other that afternoon.

It was round about this time that Cheryl realised that Africa, or what she knew of it now, had its own smell, of charcoal fires and roasted meat and maize. Just like her first few days in Paris had made her realise that France had its typical smell, of freshly-baked bread and old wine.

* * *

A few days later, Otto called her at the office again, and invited her to a nightspot some way out of Nairobi. She accepted willingly.

They ate delicious roast goat meat in the open air, sitting at rough-hewn tables, drank a lot of *Tusker baridi*, and danced to an excellent Congolese band. Cheryl barely noticed the mosquitoes.

When it was time to go back to town, Cheryl realised that having first fallen in love with Paris, she had now fallen in love with Africa. She also knew what was coming next, having decided to let matters take their apparently natural course.

She told Otto that they could not go back to her single room at The Excalibur, so he took her to the Green Door Bar and Lodging House for the night, an establishment on Nairobi's River Road that he evidently already knew.

* * *

In Paris, the *intersyndicale* was busy with the details of the strike ballot, scrupulously recording the results of the votes cast in the agency's dozens of foreign and provincial bureaux as they came in by telephone or the service notes wire.

Unknown to the trade unions, unknown even to the managing director and his friend the finance minister, both the prime minister's office and the foreign affairs ministry had begun to take a quiet interest in the crisis at France-Dépêches, through their representatives on the agency's administrative board.

The administrative board was scheduled to meet in a few days' time to consider Managing Director Christophe

Juliet's controversial 'action plan', but by common consent within the corridors of power – no doubt due to the discreet intervention of the prime minister's office and the Quai d'Orsay – the session was put back by a full month.

After continued publicity about the crisis in the agency – and notably about the strike ballot, whose likely outcome no-one dared to predict – the prevailing view in the PM's entourage was that there was no need to proceed with haste in adopting the Juliet plan, no need to inflame the situation and court more adverse publicity at this stage.

Juliet and Finance Minister Delachasse were perhaps just a touch too avid and insensitive, the prime minister's office let it be known to selected representatives of the Parisian and regional press groups on the agency's administrative board.

Of course, the government was united on the principles behind the plan for the agency, just as it had been regarding the privatisation of a number of other public or semi-public enterprises. That much was made clear to these press group interests by the PM's men.

But the prime minister's private advisors had expressed doubts to him as to whether the lucrative potential of France-Dépêches was sufficient to justify the political risks of the operation. A cautious man, whose political prudence had served him well so far, he was inclined to accept their view.

If they had been paying more attention, Managing Director Juliet and his friend the finance minister would have got the message and reined in their horses at this stage.

Work at France-Dépêches, meanwhile, went ahead more or less as usual. For unlike a traditional newspaper, or even many radio stations, a big international news agency never sleeps. Apprentice agency journalists are taught to understand early on that it's always a news deadline for some client somewhere.

Thus hundreds of journalists of all nationalities, strategically posted around the nerve centres and hotspots of the world, continued with their daily task of gathering the news, writing their copy or 'tasting' that of their colleagues, editing it and re-despatching it onto the newswires in suitably packaged form for the agency's variety of print, broadcast media and other clients.

The director of news, goaded by the ambitious and abrasive Ventrex, was predictably still unhappy with the production of the Santa de Costa bureau and its coverage of the revolution under way in that country.

"Can we please have an explanation in the copy of what is meant by a Constituent Assembly? Why is it so important, why are there these calls to hold one and at the same time so much opposition to it. Why should the State Department care about a Constituent Assembly in Santa de Costa?" he wrote in a tetchy service note to the unhappy Jean-François Cardenal.

These were questions which the regional bureau chief found he needed to put to the office's local-hire staff members, for the political ramifications of the situation had so far bypassed him. Even when the local staff patiently explained things to him, he was still not too clear.

What Jean-François did understand, however, from some of her off-hand but bitter comments, was that his normally calm and sweet-tempered 'better half', the beautiful banker's daughter Constanza, was now, for all her church-going and charitable do-gooding, to be counted among the visceral opponents of the revolution in Santa de Costa.

CHAPTER 13

Woken by strong sunshine on her face, Cheryl needed a few seconds to orient herself in the strange, bare room: there were no curtains on the window, the sheets and blankets were worn and grey, and there was a smell of dust and stuffiness. The long black form of Otelo snored softly beside her.

Too hot, Cheryl threw the bedclothes back and rolled onto her stomach, waking her partner in the process. He mumbled something, then gave a short cry of wonder. Otto had just found the small multi-coloured butterfly etched high up on her dimpled left buttock. He'd evidently not seen it during their love-making the previous night.

"What does it mean?" he asked.

"It means that you're a lucky fellow to know me this well already!"

Cheryl had the tattoo done during her last year in college. It had been the fashion among students of her age. But her reply to Otto was intended to assert herself against any complacency on his part, now that she had 'given herself to him', now that they had consummated their relationship. For Cheryl sensed a certain *machismo* in Otelo, a typically male arrogance. She found it both exciting and irritating.

To both her own surprise and his, and evidently still riding the same wave of natural impulse of the previous night, Cheryl then boldly took the sexual initiative and gave a creditable practical demonstration of the art of fellatio that left them both pleased, proud and speechless.

Impressed as he was by her hardiness, not to mention her apparent expertise in the matter, Otelo knew better than to make the slightest comment. He just lay there, breathing deeply and running an idle index finger around the nipples of her rosy big breasts, a distant smile on his face.

He could not know the extent to which Cheryl had surprised herself in this domain in the few days since she had met Otto.

For a good long while, neither of them spoke a word, and scarcely moved a limb, until the dusty heat of the bare room, overfilled with bright sunlight, drove them out into the tatty hotel corridor in search of a cool shower.

Walking up Moi Avenue together to the Nairobi city centre, Cheryl felt over-dressed and languid. They barely spoke or even touched each other further until it was time to part, when he hoarsely whispered a promise to get in touch again soon.

"Yes, do," she replied.

It seemed the time was right for both of them for some sober solitude.

* * *

When Cheryl got back to the bureau, she had a discussion with Andy Mitchell and Henri Laborie about the situation in the agency. The matter was immediately relevant, as the Nairobi bureau, like many others, still had to carry out the secret ballot of staff members on the strike call and transmit the results to Paris.

Cheryl considered herself a moderate left-winger, or 'leftist' as they tended to say in her circles on the other side of the Atlantic. True to her upbringing and inclination, reinforced by what she had so far seen of the world, she had a natural sympathy for the oppressed, the exploited and the underprivileged.

She was a staunch opponent of the US-led military wars of occupation in Iraq and Afghanistan, just as her parents' generation had opposed the Vietnam war. She was disappointed that President Barack Obama had pursued more or less the same policies as the execrated previous US president, George W. Bush. And she had been aghast at the prospect of the reactionary Republican Mitt Romney replacing Obama.

Cheryl considered herself a supporter of human rights. But like many of her age and middle-class background, she had little knowledge of social history, little experience of the organised labour movement, its trade unions and parties, its traditions, methods and aspirations.

She had been bewildered by the plethora of parties and trade union bodies in France, and by the back-biting and posturing of their leaders. She had come to perceive France-Dépêches as a microcosm of all that. She had certainly never considered joining this or that trade union. Not that she had been invited to.

Like many of her colleagues in the agency, Cheryl was also confused by the arguments for or against privatisation, the proposed modification of the agency charter, the government's drive for profitability and elimination of state subsidies. To her, it could only be a bad thing if France-Dépêches was regarded as a state enterprise and had to rely on state 'handouts'.

Andy, who had a reputation as a left-wing firebrand but had ceased union and political activity since being posted to Nairobi some three years earlier, took it upon himself to persuade her of the need to resist the new managing director's plans.

He gave what amounted to a speech, in the course of which he paced round the office and waved his arms about a lot. Cheryl retained only one salient point of Andy's rambling discourse.

"The example of how Mrs Thatcher and Tony Blair in Britain, through their shameful bullying and financial and ideological pressures, succeeded in curtailing the independence of the British Broadcasting Corporation, deliberately exposing it to hostile commercial forces and virtually reducing it to an establishment mouthpiece, is a warning of what will likely happen to France-Dépêches if we do not resist!"

My, how cute he is! A typical Englishman, and yet using such Gallic terms and gestures! Cheryl thought to herself.

Henri, by contrast, took pains to explain the issues at stake as neutrally as possible. But while declaring himself an anarchist and individualist by nature, one gathered from his summary of the situation that he too was persuaded of the need to resist Juliet's 'action plan'.

Bernard Rainier, the bureau chief, had returned to work after his illness but was still convalescent, the whites of his eyes an unhealthy yellow. He took no part in the discussion but looked on and listened into the debate through the open door of his vast office.

Andy and Henri wrote out some ballot papers for themselves, Cheryl and the bureau chief, and the four of them each marked his or her choice on them, crumpled the papers up and threw them into an empty carton. Henri then invited Cheryl to shake the carton before opening each paper and to give the result of the vote.

"Three votes in favour of the strike, one blank," she announced.

Henri promptly put the result into a short service note for the *intersyndicale*.

* * *

After yet more bullying from Ventrex, who had evidently allowed visions of himself as imminent strike leader go to his head, and after continued unsatisfactory performance from the Santa de Costa bureau, the director of news was at the end of his tether. Whatever the outcome of the crisis in the agency, he was about ready to quit the job.

"I don't think I can stand much more of this," he had been repeating to himself for several days now.

The previous night he had confided to his wife Solange that he wanted to quit as director of news.

"How would you like it if I took another foreign posting?" he asked her.

"Where this time, Edouard?" she asked warily.

Solange had not enjoyed their life during his previous postings, to The Hague, New Delhi and Cairo.

"I don't know. Like Santa de Costa for example?"

"Is it coming up?"

"Not for the moment. But we may recall Cardenal.

He's making a mess of it and it's an interesting post. And Ventrex is after my job."

"But you don't speak Spanish, do you?"

"Enough to get by. Anyway, I can always brush it up. So long as the number two is competent, I could handle it. And Pierre Grangier is alright."

"But will they give it to you?"

"Normally, it would be mine if I wanted it. But who knows now, given the present situation."

They left the matter there for that night.

CHAPTER 14

As soon as the deadline of midnight on 31 October fixed by the *intersyndicale* for the close of voting arrived, two officials of each of the four unions, and eight non-union personnel chosen as independent observers, began the task of counting the votes. The operation took place in the staff canteen, Place de l'Horloge, and lasted several hours, after repeated recounts and verifications demanded by various persons.

The outcome of the ballot, according to a communiqué sent out by special service note to all of the agency's bureaux and services at home and abroad at 0600 hours Paris time the following morning, was as follows:

Number of staff eligible to vote: 1,891

Number of votes cast: 1,782

Votes in favour of the strike call: 965

Votes against: 750

Blank and spoiled votes: 67

Taking into account only the valid votes cast, this gave 54.2% in favour, 42.1% against and just 3.7% for the 'don't knows' and spoilt ballots.

The trade unions at France-Dépêches could thus reasonably consider that, as a result of democratic decision, they possessed a clear mandate for a 24-hour renewable strike on all the news-wires from 0001 hours on 15 November Paris time – unless the managing director withdrew his so-called action plan before then.

The result of the vote was relayed to the finance ministry, the foreign ministry and the prime minister's office by 0800 hours that morning and by 0900 hours the news of a strike threat at France-Dépêches was being carried on all the main French radio stations.

The French news agency's two main international rivals, Amalgamated News and Beckers, each carried a report of the development on their news-wires. Though in the main factual in their accounts, the two Anglo-American agencies referred perfidiously to France-Dépêches as 'the French state news agency', thereby casting implicit doubt on its present independent status.

France-Dépêches gave the news of the strike threat on its own wires in despatches on all the French and foreign language wires that were a model of news agency sobriety and neutrality.

Here is how the English-language wires rendered the news:

French news agency staff vote to strike against jobs cut plan

PARIS, 1 November – Staff of the international news agency France-Dépêches have voted to strike unless management withdraws a government-backed austerity and part-privatisation plan, trade union sources said Monday.

A new managing director installed at the agency by France's recently-elected right-wing government wants to cut staff numbers by about a third – from a present 1,900 to around 1,200 – and amend the agency's governing charter in order to sell shares in it.

If his plan were put into effect, up to 49% of the share capital would be sold to investors, with the French state retaining a majority holding.

But in a trade union-organised ballot following three weeks of deadlocked talks, journalists, administrative and technical staff at the agency have voted to strike as of 15 November if the 'action plan' of Chief Executive Christophe Juliet is not withdrawn, the sources said.

In a secret ballot, 54% of the staff voted in favour of the strike, with 42% against and less than 4% 'don't knows', a joint statement issued by the unions said.

If the strike were to go ahead, it would be the first time in over sixty years of its existence that such action has halted the flow of news to the French agency's clients.

Opponents of the government-backed 'action plan' say that jobs must be preserved and that the plan threatens the agency's independence, but its backers say the agency must cut costs and attract investment in order to meet the challenges of the digital age.

The 'action plan' is in line with the French government's aim of phasing out all subsidies to public enterprises within the next two years, in conformity with directives from Brussels under the European Union's Maastricht and Lisbon treaties aimed at ensuring free competition.

France-Dépêches is the world's third-biggest news agency, after Becker's and Amalgamated Press. Unlike its two Anglo-American rivals, it relies on state subsidies to maintain its global news network, although a 1946 founding charter guarantees its independence.

In a public statement, Christophe Juliet expressed his *"deep regret that the personnel of France-Dépêches have chosen to follow the trade unions on their path of confrontation rather than consensus.*

"I appeal to all members of staff, and particularly their representatives, even at this stage, to reconsider their position. In conformity with my mandate and with the pressing need to modernise France-Dépêches, I have sought solutions which I think serve the general interest best," the statement went on.

"I understand the legitimate concerns and anxieties of members of staff, and I remain ready to meet their representatives at any time in an attempt to find solutions which could provide the necessary reassurances.

"The very last thing the agency and all of its staff need now is the threat of a strike, which can only further worsen the agency's commercial and competitive situation."

If the managing director had hoped thereby to alter the course of events, it was a forlorn hope. His statement, full of pathos as it was, seemed on closer examination simply to be aimed at saving face and playing for time.

The *intersyndicale* promptly responded with a statement which *"welcomed the managing director's acknowledgement of the legitimate concerns of the staff in the face of the threat posed by his 'action plan'.*

"However, the unions note that Mr Juliet has still not withdrawn his unacceptable plan, which means that any negotiation or consultation supposedly aimed at reassuring staff members in the light of their legitimate concerns remains impossible," the statement added.

"This being the case, the intersyndicale *maintains its call for a 24-hour strike on all news-wires for 15 November."*

Separately, the *intersyndicale* announced that a further mass meeting would be held in the agency's Paris headquarters on 7 November.

* * *

The next ninety-six hours saw a frenzy of behind-the-scenes activity in a bid to resolve the crisis before the strike deadline, and if possible before the 7 November mass meeting of agency staff.

The hyper-active Ventrex spent hours on the telephone speaking to senior members of the Socialist Party, urging them to intercede via the prime minister's office.

The two minority trade unions represented in France-Dépêches urgently sought discreet audience with the managing director, notwithstanding the public relations risk of such a move. Evidently blind to the danger to the agency's independence from Juliet's plan, they intimated to him that they too believed a change in the founding charter was needed in order to attract private investment.

The present situation, however, would not allow immediate acceptance of such a change, they warned. They advised Juliet that he should leave this part of the plan aside for the meanwhile. They pleaded with him instead to increase the number of new job creations to offset the seven hundred or so that were expected to be lost according to the plan.

Appreciative of their efforts, Juliet promised that he would try his best to increase the new job creations beyond the fifteen to twenty he had already mentioned, if that would win their tacit collaboration regarding the expected job losses. But within forty-eight hours of the strike ballot results being made public, the managing director committed a tactical error.

On his own initiative, he had published in a leading French financial newspaper an article signed by himself which attacked the trade unions at France-Dépêches for their *"archaism"* and their *"obstructionism in the face of necessary modernisation"*. The article also claimed that the strike vote had been carried *"only by a narrow majority"*.

The Juliet article – which no doubt had the approval of Juliet's highly-placed old friend, Finance Minister Delachasse, if the man had not actually directly inspired it – made no difference to the majority unions led by Gareth Galant and Paul Ventrex. For them, the die was cast, the countdown to a strike had begun, and only the withdrawal of Juliet's 'action plan' could now halt it

However, if the purpose of the article had been to weaken the trade unions' position, its aggressive tone was counter-productive, tending rather to convince some of the undecided elements among agency staff members that the threat of a strike was indeed the only possible recourse.

That the millionaire owner of the financial paper which ran the article was represented on the France-Dépêches administrative board was a further factor in the uneasy situation, though how exactly no-one was quite able or willing to say.

In a joint public statement signed by Ventrex and Galant, the General Union and the Democratic Union journalists' sections at the agency seized upon the article written by Juliet as evidence of the managing director's *"bad faith and confrontational attitude"*.

"Mr Juliet seems still not to understand the situation which he himself has created and which he must now resolve by drawing the only possible logical conclusion, that is, he must unconditionally withdraw his 'action plan'."

The fact that the two minority journalists' unions at the agency had not signed this statement was noted in follow-up articles carried by the mainstream French daily press the following day.

The Juliet article also infuriated the prime minister, who sensed a further danger brewing for the government. An occasional journalist and broadcaster himself in his younger days, he knew something of the perils for politicians who meddled with the media.

The article added to his secret contempt for the brash finance minister and his *protégé* Christophe Juliet. The two reflected the arrogant yuppie-like neo-conservative political style of the Head of State in whose service he found himself, rather than his own more old-fashioned approach.

Harried by representations both from opposition members of parliament and members of the ruling majority regarding the crisis at France-Dépêches, and in the midst of a number of other no-less-serious conflicts of the government's own making, the PM convened a meeting devoted to the agency in his Matignon office for 5 November.

Summoned were both Juliet and Delachasse, as well as a senior representative of the foreign ministry, the PM's own chief press and public relations adviser, his special advisor for privatisations and his special advisor for relations with parliament.

On the basis of his own instincts and what his advisors had been able to tell him, the prime minister wanted the controversial plan for the news agency put on the back burner, given all the other problems the government had.

Subsequent events would seem to confirm the PM's instincts. It was his bad luck that a political scandal which had been brewing for several weeks now suddenly burst into the open, severely shaking the government at a moment when it was already embattled on other fronts.

As often in the past with scandals involving French governments, whether of right-wing or left-wing complexion, this one began with an article in the satirical weekly newspaper *Le Canard Enchaîné*.

Le Canard revealed that the justice minister, Dominic Carnot, had been accused of rape and sexual assault by a secretary employed in the rural municipality of which he had been mayor for the last thirteen years. Carnot vigorously denied the accusations levelled by the secretary, with whom he apparently had had a brief love affair before their relations went seriously wrong.

The allegations related to a period several years ago,

well before Carnot was named justice minister and while his party, the Union of French Citizens (UFC), was in opposition at national level.

The allegations were in themselves serious enough. But worse still, according to *Le Canard Enchaîné*, Carnot had offered a four-figure sum of money to the secretary if she would withdraw them. When that failed to dissuade her, Carnot allegedly sought to pressure the regional prosecutor not to open an investigation. In vain.

On the morning of 5 November, the regional prosecutor's office announced that, following investigation, Carnot had a case to answer and should stand trial. The prime minister found himself, after urgent consultation with the President, having to accept the resignation of the justice minister.

Thus it was that the meeting which was to have taken place that afternoon in the prime minister's office on the situation at France-Dépêches was first postponed and then cancelled, when the PM was called upon to make a statement in parliament on the Carnot affair, upon which the opposition parties had been insisting.

The PM kept his statement to the strict minimum, hiding behind the need not to comment on a matter now before the courts. But the affair still ballooned out of control rapidly, with further press reports to the effect that leaders of the Union of French Citizens in the minister's home region had long been aware of a number of similar allegations concerning Carnot.

And if leaders of the President's own political party in the central Auvergne province had long been aware of the justice minister's reputation as a dangerously irrepressible satyr, did this imply that quite possibly national leaders of the UFC were aware of them too? Just how much did the President himself therefore know and apparently cover up, for that matter?

CHAPTER 15

The situation at France-Dépêches was thus allowed to go to the brink, and beyond. With the government badly shaken and distracted by the Carnot sex-offence scandal, on top of mounting social tensions in the country caused by the government's provocative right-wing economic policies, it seemed that nothing was now able to prevent the festering conflict at France-Dépêches coming to the final crunch.

Tension at the agency was at an all-time high, and the battle lines were drawn. The 7 November mass meeting came and went with no apparent change in the deadlocked situation. The trade unions said that Juliet had given no indication that he was prepared to withdraw his plan. The strike was still scheduled to go ahead as of 15 November.

This mass meeting was a fraught affair, however. Ventrex was repeatedly interrupted from the floor during his report on the situation, and when Galant intervened in order to back up his colleague's interpretation of events, the trade union officers all but lost control of the situation in the face of catcalls from so-called moderates deeply opposed to a strike.

The two, backed by some unexpected eleventh-hour supporters who suddenly discovered their class consciousness at this late stage, managed to head off an inept attempt to force through a motion calling for a "cooling-off period of seven days", to be followed by a "renewal of trade union-management contacts without pre-conditions".

Juliet, for his part, sent a signed letter to all of the agency's employees laying out the reasons for his 'action plan' and expressing the hope that *"even at this stage, reason will prevail"*.

"My door remains open for unconditional talks at any time with any or all of the parties concerned to try to resolve this conflict in a reasonable manner," he wrote.

A complicating new factor now entered the equation. On the evening of 7 November – that is, on the same day as the mass meeting, but well after its close – all the agency's bureaux and services were informed by a special service note of the creation of an 'Association of France-Dépêches Journalists' claiming to be independent of both the trade unions and Juliet and his team.

The text of the announcement, which was pinned up on all office noticeboards, said that the situation had *"been allowed to go too far"*, as a strike could only further harm the agency's image and competitive position.

"We understand the fears expressed by the trade unions regarding the independence of the agency and the prospect of job losses. However, we also regret that the managing director's action plan has so far been rejected out of hand by the trade unions, given that it contains some positive or

useful elements. We believe that a way must be found to try to build upon these elements in order to save the agency and the jobs of its employees. We call upon all journalist staff members who share this view to join the Association to help enable free democratic debate of all the issues at stake."

The clearly mischievous implication was that free democratic debate of the issues at stake had somehow been stifled up until now.

Judging by the names given as constituting the pompous-sounding 'provisional council' of the 'Association of France-Dépêches Journalists', this was an initiative which had strong support among service chiefs and deputy chiefs, so-called middle-management.

Among the five named leaders of this 'Association of France-Dépêches Journalists' was Russell McCarthy, a former head of the English Service and former White House correspondent, who had recently been named Hong Kong regional bureau chief, in overall charge of all Asian English-language coverage.

McCarthy was something of a 'golden boy' in the agency, in that he had been largely responsible for improving the English-language services in recent years, to the point where France-Dépêches could seriously compete with Amalgamated Press and Beckers. With his ginger beard, nervous tics and machine-gun speech delivery, McCarthy was a caricature of the energetic hard-news reporter, and a brash New Yorker to boot. He had risen rapidly to management level within the agency due to his dynamism and uncompromising professionalism.

As a fellow American, but from Boston, remarked to one of her English desk colleagues: "You wouldn't want to spend too much time in the same room as him. Apart from the fact that he's a typically pushy New Yorker, he really is so hyper that he's just a bit too much."

And as one old hand had quipped to colleagues when McCarthy first arrived on the English desk some years earlier, "I know he's very good because he told me so himself!"

McCarthy had been one of the most vociferous opponents of the strike at the rowdy 7 November mass meeting, and there was no doubt that his views carried a certain amount of weight.

Galant, who had been expecting a manoeuvre of this kind, convened a new meeting of all Democratic Union staff members for the following Monday. He would also have liked to talk to Paul Ventrex, to know his view of this latest development, but was unable to reach him. Ventrex was not answering his mobile phone and nobody knew where he was to be found.

CHAPTER 16

Waking with yet another *Tusker baridi* hangover, to find a large and no-longer-young African woman snoring in his bed, Andy Mitchell told himself, not for the first time, that he really must stop drinking so much. He reflected that it would be better, for his moral and physical health, to cease frequenting loose women.

Andy then panicked for a moment, entirely unable to remember how he had got home, and wondered where he had left his MG sports car. Wrapping a Maasai-style *kikoi* about himself, he teetered to the front door and looked out onto the drive. To his relief, the vehicle was standing there under the banana palms, albeit with its headlights apparently still on.

"Ho hum," he said vacuously to himself. "Battery's probably flat by now. Still, at least I'm still alive. Could be worse!"

Odwori sidled up to him as he made his way back to the bedroom.

"Want bleckfast, Mr Andy?"

"Yes please, Odwori, bleckfast for two."

Andy wondered whether it was not time to follow his father's advice and get married, or at least find a nice girl and settle down to a steadier life. Not for the first time, he toyed with the notion of 'going native' and going to live in northern Kenya, somewhere near the Ethiopian border, or perhaps in a Somali region. Or working as a freelance out of Mombasa.

His mind drifted back to Njoki, as he remembered her pretty little breasts and sweet nature, and he felt a pang of loneliness and regret. Why had he not tried to see her again, instead of picking up a doubtful creature like the one he presently found himself with? He resolved to seek Njoki out.

Meanwhile, he had to get it together to go to the office. It was a Sunday, and it was his turn to man the bureau that day so as to give the other staffers a day off. Embarrassingly, he had to ask Odwori to help him bump-start the car.

Driving excessively slowly along the dual carriageway leading to the city centre, he was overtaken on the wrong side by two Asians in a large recent BMW who hooted and shook their fists at him. Furious, he flashed the middle-finger sign and honked his horn back at them, before realising that he was in the wrong because he had been driving in the overtaking lane. Despite his life-long love of motorcars, Andy was not a very good driver, and prone to occasional so-called 'road-rage'.

He was still bleary and hung over when he got to the office and Matt handed him a service note emanating from the London bureau which Paris had passed on. One of the more lurid British tabloids, *The Star on Sunday*, had splashed a story headlined 'Brits in deadly 'safari bug' horror'. Could Nairobi check it out?

The story, attributed to an unnamed '*Star on Sunday* staff correspondent', claimed that five British tourists on a Kenyan game park tour were "believed infected with a deadly viral plague which has already killed hundreds of Africans", and that they had been quarantined in a private Nairobi clinic, also unnamed.

"*Fuck, fuck, fuck!*" was all Andy could think and say for a full five minutes. Where to begin, on a Sunday too? So far as Andy knew, there was certainly no '*Sunday Star* correspondent' in Nairobi. Nor could he guess which medical establishment could be described as a private clinic, but phoned the city's two main hospitals to see if they knew anything.

Of course, no-one could help. He even phoned at his home an Italian tropical diseases doctor who'd treated him for hepatitis contracted in Addis Ababa two years earlier. The man would have liked to help, he said, but knew nothing either.

Andy then forced himself to phone the British high commissioner's residence, but found his call immediately routed to the consulate.

The British diplomats in Nairobi were waspish at the

best of times, Andy had found, at least where France-Dépêches was concerned. He attributed this to an age-old hostility between the English and the French and suspected the high commission of being more helpful to British media representatives than others.

But he was in luck this time: the consulate had prepared a statement on the matter. The spokesman said that five British subjects had indeed been examined at the Aga Khan hospital; four of them had been discharged and the fifth had been emergency airlifted to Johannesburg. End of statement. No names or other details.

Andy duly wrote and sent a service note 'attn Joburg' passing this information on, and supposed the matter now disposed of, or at least to be off the bureau's territory. Unfortunately for him, and even more so for the infected British tourist, the latter was dead on arrival at South Africa's Oliver Tambo airport.

A correspondent of the German news agency broke that news to Andy. Dieter Kühn phoned him, having been alerted by Berlin and Hamburg that two German tabloids were going to run a story in their Monday editions on "the first European victim of African viral plague" and already had it on their websites.

Andy then received a call from the acting chief news editor in Paris, who first asked to speak to the bureau chief, and appeared surprised that he was not in the office. Andy had been too preoccupied even to think of calling

Rainier, but hurriedly did so now, telling him what copy Paris wanted produced as soon as possible.

This was, he relayed to his boss, six hundred words in French and in English of the latest hard news, datelined Nairobi but incorporating input from Jo'burg and London, plus a five-hundred-word calendar of events since the first outbreak of the disease, also in both languages, by 1000 GMT, with the same items updated or refreshed for 1230 GMT.

The request was confirmed a few minutes later by a service note, which added that Geneva was providing four hundred words of updated WHO-based information about the viral plague.

At this point Andy phoned Rainier again to suggest that Cheryl or Henri Laborie be mobilised too. "Don't tell me how to do my job," the bureau chief snapped back, then had the nerve to ask Andy to summon the other two himself, which he did. Within an hour, both arrived in the office, followed a half-hour later by Rainier himself.

Sunday suddenly became a busy working day for the whole Nairobi press corps simply because one white European had died of a terrible disease which had already killed thousands of black Africans.

As for the East African safari tour operators, already hard-hit by the economic crisis, they could shut down entirely now.

CHAPTER 17

After a frustratingly futile weekend of worrying about where the conflict was headed, Galant finally succeeded in getting Ventrex on the phone the following Monday, only a half-hour before the emergency meeting of the Democratic Union sections which he had convened.

The conversation began unsatisfactorily from Galant's point of view. Ventrex, who was still mysteriously absent from the agency's premises, seemed unusually distant and guarded in his replies. Galant once again had the impression that his long-time rival had no stomach for the fight that was shaping up.

He guessed that Ventrex was working hard behind the scenes, using his Socialist Party contacts, to try to defuse the situation. Though how he hoped to achieve anything, given the unbending position of Juliet and the apparent support he had in the government, seemed very doubtful.

While Galant had been expecting something of the sort, he was nevertheless worried by the sudden appearance of the pro-management 'Association of France-Dépêches Journalists' at this critical juncture. It was, he told Ventrex, a manoeuvre aimed at undermining the democratic process over which the trade unions had presided.

"The ultimate purpose is to allow all or part of Juliet's

'action plan' to go through, and it should therefore be denounced for what it is," he told Ventrex.

Galant proposed that the Democratic Union and General Union issue a joint statement to this effect, if possible together with the minority unions. Ventrex was not keen, however, replying that this could only inflame passions and risked dividing the staff further rather than uniting them.

Galant realised then that his arch-rival was probably right this time, and that this was not the time to charge ahead on that front. He was secretly grateful to Ventrex for this.

"Can you tell me where you are at this moment, Paul?" he asked.

Galant had put the question out of pure curiosity. He had no special need or right to know where Ventrex was or what he was up to, and was conscious that the question was indiscreet.

"Gareth, I am in the private office of Jean-Jacques Restant, if you must know."

J-J R, as he was familiarly known, was a former minister of the interior and a leading member of the Socialist Party. During his time in office he had been a highly valuable source of information for Ventrex in the latter's capacity as head of the agency's home news service.

J-J R was on the right-wing of the Socialist Party, however, and could hardly be considered a friend of the trade union movement.

The revelation by Ventrex of his whereabouts was a reminder to both men of the important political differences which separated them: Ventrex, the Socialist Party member with personal contacts in high places, Galant, the Trotskyist with only his trade union position for a social base.

Galant supposed that Ventrex was in Restant's office as much to cultivate his professional contact as a journalist with the former minister, as in connection with the acute crisis at France-Dépêches. On the other hand, one could not really know; Ventrex was notoriously fond of behind-the-scenes wheeler-dealering.

Galant thanked Ventrex for his advice and apologised for having disturbed him before hanging up.

After a brief discussion with Marie-Claude and two other Democratic Union militants at the agency, Galant resolved simply to provide an analysis of the situation to the meeting, which he kept brief. Galant said that the creation of a 'so-called Association of France-Dépêches Journalists' was intended to undermine and counter the position of the trade unions at a critical moment.

"The trade unions must stay firm at this point. There can be no shift from the position which the personnel have confirmed by a democratic vote – that is, unless Juliet unconditionally withdraws his unacceptable 'action plan' there will be an all-out strike by agency personnel beginning on 15 November. Can I take it that we are all agreed on this?"

A murmur of assent assured him that this was so. There was not the trace of a dissenting voice.

Underlining that there had been no indication whatsoever from Juliet that the management position had altered in any way, Galant closed the meeting.

Somewhat ostentatiously, he then immediately telephoned Ventrex again, in front of those colleagues who were still present, to inform the General Union leader that the DU personnel were, despite the 'Association of Journalists' manoeuvre, ready to go on strike if the 'action plan' was not abandoned.

"I thought you would like to know," Galant told him and hung up. The strike deadline of 15 November was only five days away and approaching fast.

CHAPTER 18

Despite drinking regularly of an evening in the Rainbow Bar, Andy had been disappointed at not finding Njoki there again. He resolved not to go with any of the other girls from the bar before tracking down the sweet little Njoki. He sent a note to her postbox with his home and office telephone numbers, asking her to get in touch if she wanted to see him again.

To his considerable joy and excitement, some four or five days later Njoki telephoned him at the office one morning and invited him to eat with her in her new lodging. Her flatmate and her flatmate's boyfriend would be there too, she said.

"Should I bring anything?" he asked.

"Just bring yourself and some beer!"

Njoki tickled his fancy terribly, Andy realised. He made a conscious effort to recall her physical appearance: small, pert and smiling, with big black eyes and long pigtails.

It took him a good hour to reach the estate of small concrete and cinder-block houses way out over the other side of town where Njoki now lived. The huge Dora Dora housing estate – Americans would call it a project – was socially just a cut above the shanty towns around Nairobi such as Karawangi, Kalisha and Kariobani.

It took him another quarter of an hour to find her street and the house. It all looked the same: drab grey-brown and dusty, with just numbers to identify the streets and letters to distinguish the low tenement blocks.

Njoki greeted him warmly and introduced him to the other guests. She and her flatmate, a leggy shock-haired Kamba girl named Irene, had made a special culinary effort. They had also dressed for the occasion in African rather than western style. The two young women both wore brightly coloured *kangas* – Njoki's was yellow and black, Irene's red and black – together with rustic leather sandals and a mass of beads and copper bangles.

Dinner was composed of a spicy goat-meat stew with rice, green bananas fried in *ghee* (butter oil), red beans and *sukuma wiki*, a kind of kale or cabbage. Plus, of course, the inevitable Tusker beer.

Irene's boyfriend was introduced as Kamau, a grave-faced young Kikuyu who worked as a draughtsman for a firm of Nairobi architects.

"I have good news, Andy," Njoki announced as they began to eat.

She explained that she had obtained a job as a trainee bank employee, thanks to the influence of her father's family, whom she had been visiting in Nyeri for the past two weeks. Her father had also helped her obtain the two-roomed ground-floor apartment that she shared with Irene.

Andy was genuinely happy for her. However, he was also beginning to desire her intensely, which she obviously realised and encouraged. She repeatedly caught his hand and smiled at him, and once let her *kanga* fall open to reveal her small round breasts, as they all sat in a row on a makeshift sofa made of packing cases, drinking beer after the meal.

Andy was hoping and expecting to have sex with Njoki that night. He was therefore disappointed when the two girls said that he and Kamau would have to leave soon, as the landlord had forbidden them from entertaining men at night.

"He will say we are prostitutes and throw us out," Irene explained.

After giving Njoki a date to meet in the Rainbow Bar the following week, Andy left with Kamau. He gave Kamau a lift to the other side of Dora Dora before driving home to Westlands in his old MG, still relatively sober, for a rare early night to bed.

CHAPTER 19

Poor Jean-François Cardenal! Life had not been all plain sailing for him lately. His wife Constanza was constantly on the phone to her rich lady friends, who complained to each other about the misdeeds of the 'communist government' of President Lopez. Although there had so far been absolutely no question of this, she evidently feared that the banks, including her father's, would be nationalised.

The director of news kept harrying him with service notes, and he was having trouble keeping up with the political situation in his region. He still needed to ask the local-hire journalists the significance of various events, and yet when they explained them to him, he remained sceptical and unsatisfied, uncomprehending. His leisurely lifestyle was finished, he was now obliged to work!

Too late, he understood that he had not cultivated the right contacts in Santa de Costa. Instead of frequenting French- and Spanish-speaking diplomats or his wife's friends, he should have got to know some CIA types or think-tank people.

It frustrated and anguished him to read reports by Amalgamated Press or Beckers on the situation in Santa de Costa or the region as a whole which quoted 'US security sources' and suchlike.

He realised he was no longer enjoying his job and

wondered if it was not time to return to France. But what would the snobbish Constanza have to say if he found himself being offered a head of bureau post in 'provincial' Lille or Lyons?

Above all, Jean-François Cardenal had only imperfectly understood the geopolitical stakes of which he was a privileged witness. For outside of the Middle East, nowhere else was the struggle for news and views under sharper ideological pressure than in Central and Southern America, simply because Uncle Sam considered this region his own backyard.

Precisely because of this, France-Dépêches had long enjoyed a certain advantage over its two main rivals: the rather parochial US-dominated Amalgamated Press, and Beckers, which at heart was largely a creature of British finance capitalism.

Thanks to its apparently more independent position, and the fact that it had a strong network of correspondents and bureaux in the region, the French agency had been able to gain and keep media clients who wanted a different angle on Latin American news.

While this trump card had remained valid for the agency's Iberian clients who took its Spanish-language service, the English- and French-language services had been slow off the mark in reporting recent events in Santa de Costa, and this was a blow to France-Dépêches's credibility at a critical time.

The failure by the agency to provide important paying clients with timely informed reports of events in Santa de Costa was especially unfortunate, given that the Anglo-American media had been hostile in their coverage of the revolution there, reflecting the viewpoints of Wall Street and the City of London.

In Washington, the State Department had issued a veiled warning to neighbouring Latin American and Caribbean states not to support the seizure of foreign land holdings by the government of President Lopez and to 'remain neutral'.

US foreign policy might have changed in style with the replacement of the white Republican George W. Bush by the black Democrat Barack Obama as president, but the bottom line seemed to be the same, political observers noted. Washington in reality hoped to stifle the revolution with a veritable economic and diplomatic blockade of the country, according to these political observers.

The US government evidently feared the danger of revolutionary contagion in the sub-continent, and the old 'domino theory' was still in vogue. That at least was how Jean-François Cardenal put it in one of his pompous 'analysis' articles, and he was not entirely wrong there.

* * *

Several thousand miles away, on the other side of the world, Cheryl Keyes was in the throes of a torrid love affair of the likes she had never known.

She spent several more nights with Otelo Okello in the large dusty hotel room in Nairobi's notorious River Road where they had first made love and found herself hungrily looking forward to their trysts. Their long nights of lovemaking aroused a sexual side to her character that she had never came close to imagining or realising in her years with David.

Otto, she learned, had a standing arrangement with the proprietor of the Green Door Bar and Lodging House: when he was alone, he took a tiny room there on a back landing scarcely bigger than a broom cupboard; the big room was his for when he took her back there.

Although Otto was scrupulously gentlemanly in his treatment of her, Cheryl's starry-eyed love for him took a blow the night she learned that he would shortly be leaving Nairobi, but not returning directly to his editorial office in Dakar.

He would, he told her with ill-concealed shame, first be visiting his Acholi tribe wife and their child in Gulu town, in northern Uganda, as it was high time that he provided them with money for corn meal, clothes, shoes and school fees. He did not see them often, he confessed.

Cheryl knew she should have guessed that a man like Otto could not have reached his age – he said he was thirty-six – without having acquired some moral baggage of that sort. But she was nevertheless shaken by the revelation.

She was still in a state of emotional shock when she learned from the regional bureau chief Bertrand Rainier the following morning that she was being recalled to Paris. A seat had already been reserved for her on a plane leaving in thirty-six hours' time.

The 'mystery disease' story was winding down, the bureau chief told her, with the number of new infections reported in recent days down to single figures. Whether this was due to the vaccination campaign or general preventive measures was not clear. In any event, it seemed that Bernard Rainier had succeeded in getting Cheryl recalled.

However, she then learned from Andy that the bureau was sending Henri Laborie to the East African coast for an update on the situation there and a possible visit to the Omarou islands. So much for the story 'winding down' then!

Cheryl and Otto would have to go their separate ways, she realised with a heavy heart, although he promised solemnly to stay in close touch with her.

"Can you come and visit me in Dakar, Senegal?" Otto asked.

She barely had the heart to tell him he was being unrealistic, that she had a job to do in Paris.

"Then I'll come and visit you in Paris."

"That would be nice."

Cheryl was too dispirited to say anything more but gave him a brave smile.

They embraced and parted, he by a series of buses and *matatus* (bush taxis) to Gulu town, she back to the 18th *arrondissement* of Paris via Jomo Kenyatta airport and Orly airport in a lumbering Boeing 747 a day later.

Cheryl felt queasy throughout the flight and vomited her Air France in-flight dinner.

She had been feeling poorly for a couple of days already, and also sensed that she had put on a few unwelcome extra pounds in weight during her stay in Nairobi. She attributed it to the Tusker beer and stodgy restaurant food. Cheryl had since adolescence been waging a silent battle against a tendency to put on weight.

CHAPTER 20

Unaccountably, the managing director of France-Dépêches, Christophe Juliet, seemed somehow still to believe that he would be able to impose his part-privatisation and down-sizing plan on the agency, despite the opposition of its trade unions and a majority of the staff.

There had been no direct communication between him and the unions since they had notified him of the outcome of the strike ballot a week earlier.

The government, for its part, had so many other preoccupations that the problem of France-Dépêches was currently low on its list of priorities, so there was no prospect of immediate intervention from that quarter either.

"It looks like we really are going to be on strike tomorrow," Gareth Galant confided to his beautiful red-haired mistress Marie-Claude Schroedinger on the evening of 14 November, which fell upon a Friday.

Galant and his brother-in-arms Paul Ventrex had earlier in the day successfully resisted last-ditch efforts by opponents of the strike to convene an emergency mass meeting aimed at overturning the strike decision.

Arguing that the strike had already been democratically

decided, they proposed instead that a mass meeting be held at 1700 hours the following day – that is, the Saturday – to review the situation and, eventually, to decide if the strike should be prolonged for a further twenty-four hours.

Frustrated, the opponents of the strike thereupon held a meeting in the upstairs room of a large café-restaurant near the Place de l'Horloge under the auspices of the newly-created 'Association of France-Dépêches Journalists'.

No text of any decision by this association was made public. However, according to more-or-less deliberate leaks, it was understood that a consensus had been reached by the participants, who numbered some thirty or forty. The consensus was that they should continue working during the strike and try to ensure a 'skeleton' or minimum news service.

Prominent among the participants at this meeting of volunteer strike-breakers were a number of middle-management figures and various bureau and service chiefs or their deputies. They of course included Russell McCarthy, the former English Service chief and Washington correspondent, recently named head of Asian news and to be based in Hong Kong.

"Let them try to break the strike, it's they who will look the worst for it," Galant told Marie-Claude. He was no longer worried by the situation.

"I've told Paul Ventrex that the Democratic Union will

set up pickets at the main entrance to the agency building, and our members will simply ask those entering to respect the strike. But there will be no attempt to physically prevent people going into work."

Galant was thinking rather of the next phase of the struggle, and explained to Marie-Claude what that thinking was.

"At tomorrow's mass meeting, which will review the first day of strike action, we must propose the formation of a strike committee to manage the struggle as it develops. Ideally this strike committee should comprise representatives of all four trade union confederations and some non-union members.

"The members of this strike committee should be elected by the mass meeting, which of course is open to all agency employees whatever their role or rank. You could well be a member of the strike committee, Marie-Claude.

"I also think you are the right person to make this proposal at tomorrow's mass meeting. I will back you up in the discussion which follows, as will one or two of our other comrades.

"We must expect Ventrex to oppose such a move, as will the minority unions. They will hate the idea of a strike committee, but some other members of the General Union will probably disagree with Ventrex and back us on this issue. We will have to see what happens."

Marie-Claude need not have worried at having to play a firebrand role. For it never quite came quite to that.

* * *

From 0700 hours on Saturday, 15 November, a half-dozen members of the Democratic Union, mostly journalists but including at least one former text transmission technician, now a driver-messenger as his craft had disappeared with the arrival of new technology, formed a picket line in front of the agency's headquarters building.

They bore placards proclaiming 'France-Dépêches on strike!' and 'No privatisation, no job cuts!'

By 0830 the DU members had been joined by a number of militant journalist members of the General Union. The atmosphere among them was of friendly solidarity, and none of the persons who sought to enter the building to work was harassed or impeded.

The only tense moment occurred when the chauffeur-driven limousine of Christophe Juliet arrived. The former technician Dominic planted himself in front of the vehicle before it entered the gate and shook his fist at the boss presumably inside, who was invisible behind the tinted glass.

Two DU comrades quickly grabbed Dominic by the arms and drew him gently back before the small contingent of riot police posted on the other side of the

Place de l'Horloge in evident connection with the strike could intervene. Otherwise, there was no incident.

However, the scene was filmed by a privately-owned Paris television news channel team and made for a brief dramatic Saturday lunchtime news clip on what was described as "the conflict at the state news agency France-Dépêches, where the trade unions are resisting a government-backed privatisation and job cuts plan".

The news-monitoring staff of certain interested ministries saw to it that the attention of their respective bosses was drawn to this graphic, though in reality utterly minor, incident.

Both Gareth Galant and Marie-Claude Schroedinger made an extended appearance on the picket line, but there was no sign of Paul Ventrex.

Inside the agency, all was very quiet. The news desk and production services were sparsely manned, but this was also to be expected on a Saturday. A good many staff members had a day off any way, others simply gave themselves an unpaid extra day off.

The pattern was similar in the provinces and overseas. The agency kept running, but the production and treatment of news had fallen to a trickle. The effect was especially marked as regards sports news, which is normally heaviest on a Saturday.

A laconic special service note to clients on all the

news-wires apologised to them for the reduced service due to what the management described as "a social movement called by trade unions in the agency". The service note avoided the term 'strike' and made no mention at all of the reasons behind it.

CHAPTER 21

In Nairobi, Andy Mitchell, Henri Laborie and the rest of the staff missed the agreeable company of Cheryl Keyes – all of them except the bureau chief Bertrand Rainier, of course. Cheryl had provided a welcome and much-needed feminine presence in the office.

Having Cheryl to work with was a valuable compensation for the brooding paranoia radiated by Rainier. Andy and Henri had appreciated her sense of humour. They had also been impressed by the fact of Cheryl's affair with the black African journalist Otto, of which they had learned a little.

Cheryl left for Paris before the day set for the strike, or she might have directly participated for the first time in her life in the class struggle, albeit in a small way, alongside her colleagues.

As in most other France-Dépêches foreign bureaux, the local-hire staff, in this instance the Kenyans Matt and Tom, worked as normal on that Saturday, 15 November. Not having full staff status with the agency, they were not regarded as party to the conflict with Managing Director Juliet and the French government, and so they carried out their daily tasks at the office as usual.

But Andy and Henri made a point of observing the strike call.

"It's our democratic right," Henri told the bureau chief, who simply grunted in reply.

"This could be the end of the agency and our jobs, if the strike continues," Henri told Andy over lunch in the Asian-run tea-shop on Muindi Mbingu Street which they frequented.

"Some of us will be losing our jobs anyway if Juliet's 'action plan' is adopted," Andy observed.

Henri took a long breath before replying to his English colleague and giving full rein to his Gallic anarchism.

"I tell you what: if the strike continues and it looks like the whole agency is going down the tubes, I'm not prepared just to stand by passively and let things happen. I've got a wife and child here. I think that we would be entitled to help ourselves.

"Listen to me. For example, we could try to set up a regional news agency of our own by taking over all of the agency's present East African and Indian Ocean clients. Of course, we would have to get rid of the bureau chief somehow, not only because he's such a ghastly creep, but also because of his huge salary and expenses which would be better spent divided up between the rest of the staff."

Andy was thrilled by Henri's mad plan, which he immediately began elaborating upon with enthusiasm.

"Yes, given that we are both signatories on the bureau's bank account, we could access the funds there and get our hands on the earnings from clients' subscriptions."

Andy had forgotten for the moment that most of the agency's clients in the region were badly in arrears with their payments for the France-Dépêches news-wire, and that when they did pay it was in local currency, not euros or dollars.

Cheryl – and no doubt many others in the agency – would have been shocked and amazed by the blithe irreverent fantasies of the two men.

Like most of the staff of France-Dépêches around the world, Andy and Henri were anxious to see what the first day of the strike would bring. They therefore waited in the office in order to follow the Paris mass meeting over the radio-telephone link and to watch out for service notes.

Because of the time difference between Nairobi and Paris, the mass meeting was scheduled to begin in what would be the evening for them, but there was no question of just going home at this stage without knowing what was happening.

The bureau chief was also slouching around the office, trying to look unconcerned and pretending to work as he waited for some news from Paris.

CHAPTER 22

Only after the strike got under way did the French government again turn its attention to the crisis at France-Dépêches. The strike had evidently helped concentrate a number of minds on the matter.

Paradoxically, however, with the continuing atmosphere of crisis on the national social and political front, the conflict at the agency and the reasons behind it had received less prominence in the media on the first day of the strike than it had in preceding days.

Possibly also prompted by the indirect but persistent political strings pulled behind the scenes by Paul Ventrex via his Socialist Party contacts, the prime minister again convened an urgent meeting in his office devoted to the problems of France-Dépêches for 1500 hours that Saturday afternoon. And this time the meeting actually took place.

The PM summoned, among others, the agency's Managing Director Christophe Juliet, Finance Minister Jean-Olivier Delachasse, a representative of the foreign ministry, his press and public relations advisor, his special advisor on privatisation and free competition and his advisor on relations with the parliament.

Here was one problem that he considered he could well do without!

Gritting his teeth, the head of the French government testily requested a brief *résumé* of the situation at France-Dépêches from his press and public relations advisor, then asked all the others present for their viewpoint, before putting to them the questions that were on his mind, namely:

"Is all this trouble over a news agency really worth it? What is to be gained by it? Do we not have other more pressing, problems to deal with?

"We have the school-teachers threatening to strike, the university students are blocking the faculties, the postal workers are ready to strike, the government is already unpopular over its privatisation of public services and its bail-out of the banks. Apart from which, the parliamentary legislative timetable is already impossibly over-burdened.

"I certainly can't see the senators agreeing to rush through a fundamental change in the agency's charter for the foreseeable future, given their present workload. And even if they had the time, I'm not at all sure that they would agree to the principle. It was bad enough to persuade them to legislate on the state's involvement in broadcasting.

"At least they could accept the financial argument for opening up radio and television to outside, private capital. But even I myself am not convinced of the public interest in selling parts of France-Dépêches off to foreign media conglomerates, especially on the basis of the figures that have been mentioned.

"In short, I think we should back off for now. The present confrontation seems to me just not worth it. Even if, in the long run, we will finally have to bring the agency charter in line with European treaty requirements.

"But even Brussels has other priorities right now than to worry about the status of a rather obscure organisation of which few people have heard."

No doubt the prime minister had been taking other, private advice on the situation at the agency too. In any event, his mind seemed made up.

With a characteristic arching of his neck, which showed his distinguished leonine head to full advantage as he leaned back in his seat before the huge conference table in his palatial office, the prime minister concluded with some suitably Gaullian considerations.

"As you know, gentlemen, the President is determined to liberate the spirit of free enterprise in public life – that is our mandate and the sense of our reforms. But even this purpose must be preserved and protected against overzealous or injudicious application of our principles. That is my task and concern in this matter."

The meeting over, the PM asked Juliet and Delachasse to stay behind, and proceeded to make it clear that he wanted the 'action plan' withdrawn as soon as possible. Juliet looked to his mentor the finance minister for guidance, but realised that he no longer enjoyed royal favour when Delachasse remained silent and expressionless and avoided his gaze.

"I suppose I will have to resign," said the deflated Juliet, seeming scarcely to believe that events could veer so far out of his control so quickly.

"You must do as you judge best," the PM advised.

He paused before adding: "I'm confident that you will place the interests of this administration and the country as a whole above any personal feelings or considerations."

Not for nothing did even the prime minister's worst enemies admire his elegantly perfidious tongue.

Within the hour, Ventrex learned from "an authoritative source close to the prime minister" that Juliet intended to offer his resignation to the administrative board of France-Dépêches.

That was how he gave the news to Galant by telephone. Ventrex was not on the agency premises and Galant wondered if he was in fact somewhere in the prime minister's office.

Even as the trade union leaders prepared to announce their apparent victory at the upcoming mass meeting, a hurried and brief emergency meeting of the administrative board of France-Dépêches accepted the managing director's immediate resignation.

The board appointed the deputy managing director, Francis Renaulde, as acting chief executive. The terse one-line announcement by the board made no mention of Juliet's 'action plan' which had caused all the trouble.

There was no public word from the government, be it the prrime minister's office, the finance ministry or any other ministry or department, in relation to events at France-Dépêches.

All had evidently decided to keep a low profile on the question of the future of the French news agency. Even its own news-wires gave just the bare minimum of information in the shape of a two-paragraph despatch written by some strike-breaking executive editor.

Here is how the despatch appeared on the agency's English-language news-wires.

French news agency chief resigns

PARIS, 15 November – France-Dépêches Managing Director Christophe Juliet has resigned with immediate effect, a statement from the agency's administrative board said.

The board said it had appointed Deputy Managing Director Francis Renaulde as acting chief executive.

As news agency despatches go, this one was particularly disgraceful for what it failed to mention: that the agency's personnel had been on strike in resistance to Juliet's plan to part-privatise and down-size France-Dépêches, and that this was why he had been forced to resign.

The despatch also made no mention of the crucial role of the French government. But such omissions are to be expected when journalists are prevented or discouraged from fulfilling their task of informing their readers.

The trade unions sought and obtained an immediate meeting with Renaulde to know what the position now was.

Poker-faced, Renaulde informed them that he had very little to say to them at this stage. Ventrex and Galant nevertheless vied with each other to put the big question to him.

"What," they both wanted to know, "becomes of Mr Juliet's 'action plan' now? Has it been withdrawn?"

"Good question," Renaulde replied with a wintry smile.

"Well?"

"I think you can take it that it has been withdrawn. But I have a question for you," Renaulde added, glancing from one face to another. "Will you call for an end to the strike?"

Ventrex could not resist the opportunity to jump quickly into the breach, and the other trade unionists let him speak for them all.

"I think, Mr Renaulde, that if you give us your word that the 'action plan' has been withdrawn, you can take it from us that we will recommend that the strike end this very evening."

"You have my word."

Renaulde paused before adding, almost amiably: "As I don't have very much else to say or announce to you at this point, I think I'd better let you get on with your mass meeting."

He paused again. "Just remember our clients, gentlemen. Their confidence in France-Dépêches has doubtless been seriously shaken by recent events. And without their confidence, the agency is nothing."

CHAPTER 23

The mass meeting scheduled for 1700 hours on the day of the strike was well-attended, if not so well as the previous one, and the big editorial room on the third floor where it took place was abuzz with excited voices.

Of course, the news that Juliet had resigned and that Francis Renaulde had been appointed acting managing director was already known to most of the France-based agency staff and had been reported by certain French media.

At 1707 hours the same elderly union delegate who presided at the first mass meeting a month earlier again coughed into the hand-held microphone and called the assembly to order.

"The *intersyndicale* has an announcement to make," he began hoarsely, as a loud cheer went up and people began clapping and banging on desks.

Representatives of the four main unions in the *intersyndicale*, who had not yet had the time to convene among themselves to discuss the new situation, lined up ready to speak.

First off was Ventrex, who repeated what everyone already knew, namely that Juliet had resigned and been replaced, "temporarily at least", by his deputy, Renaulde. A further short cheer went up.

He then announced "the unconditional withdrawal of the Juliet 'action plan,'" which was a bold and skilful interpretation of what Francis Renaulde had told the union delegates, and said that the representatives of the General Union were therefore recommending the resumption of normal work at 1800 hours, subject to certain conditions.

There was further loud clapping from all round the room.

"The withdrawal of the 'action plan' is a victory for common sense. This victory has been achieved thanks to the firm and responsible attitude of the agency's personnel and their representatives. We must continue to demonstrate this sense of responsibility."

Ventrex strove to sound statesmanlike. He would no doubt have adopted a positively Churchillian tone if he had had the time that day to down a couple more drinks. He added that he believed the trade unions should "seek guarantees from the government regarding the future of France-Dépêches", but did not elaborate upon this thinking.

Gareth Galant spoke next.

"The withdrawal of the 'action plan' is a victory for the united front put up by the staff together with their trade unions, and we have had proof that nothing short of strike action could have been effective in obtaining this result."

The Democratic Union was naturally also recommending

the resumption of normal work, he went on, but added that the union would "remain vigilant". "The predators have been repulsed this time, but it's not the first time they have set their sights on the agency, and it's unlikely to be the last," Galant concluded.

Representatives of the two other unions spoke briefly, professing satisfaction with the outcome of the struggle and indicating their agreement on ending the strike. The union representatives then conferred a moment among themselves, before leaving it to the elderly delegate chairing the assembly to call for order and put the formal question,

"In view of the fact that France-Dépêches management has withdrawn its 'action plan', does this assembly agree with the recommendation of the intersyndicale *that normal work should resume at 1800 hours, subject to a guarantee that no employee be penalised for having gone on strike today?"*

At which point most people in the room who were not standing got up and everyone raised an arm while calling out an unequivocal, "Yes!" Another round of applause followed, together with spontaneous hand-shakes and even some mutual back-slapping, rather untypical of usually undemonstrative journalists.

It took an hour or two before the widely-shared sense of victory and relief gave way, for some, to a feeling of emptiness and anti-climax, as everyone resumed his or her usual tasks of work or went home to more prosaic or personal matters.

Gareth Galant was satisfied that the united stand of the unions and the staff at France-Dépêches had warded off – for the time being at least – a dire threat to the agency's present form and independence.

But he felt utterly drained, morally and physically. He kept telling himself he should be more pleased, especially as he was going home to a hero's welcome in the arms of Marie-Claude, who had been showing him all the love that she could, which was like that of no other woman he'd ever known. But all Galant wanted to do was curl up in a ball and sleep.

Dog-tired when the two of them reached Marie-Claude's little apartment, he embraced her briefly and staggered into the bedroom. He would have crawled into bed fully dressed, but Marie-Claude helped him off with his clothes before whispering into his ear that there was an apparently important letter for him which had been delivered by special courier.

"Open it and read it for me."

"I'm not sure I should, it's addressed to you. It was sent by special delivery, I had to sign for it this morning after you left, on the understanding that this apartment is now your address. It looks like it's a legal matter."

Galant roused himself and took the large white envelope, which evidently came from a firm of lawyers. The letter inside informed him that his wife Agathe was suing for divorce. He didn't bother to try to understand the details; he gathered simply that Agathe was taking a hostile stance and that there was no question of an amicable settlement.

In the small hours of that same night, Galant awoke bathed in a cold sweat and felt a terrifying pain in his chest.

CHAPTER 24

Gareth Galant was emergency hospitalised with a suspected heart attack. Fortunately for him, the doctors said that there was no sign of permanent cardiac damage, but he was warned that he should quit smoking immediately and rest for two weeks.

Fortunately for him too, Marie-Claude Schroedinger proved to be a perfect ministering angel, providing him with the relaxed supportive environment that he needed, while assuring him of her undying love. After a 48-hour stay in hospital, he was discharged and placed himself in her care.

Marie-Claude resolved soon after this happily short-lived crisis on the domestic front that she would concentrate more on her professional career and a little less on politics and trade union affairs in future. She decided to start learning Russian with a view to applying for a posting to the Moscow bureau.

While in no way disagreeing with the policies or practices of Workers Power, and deeply admiring Gareth Galant's commitment to the struggle, she had come to the conclusion that the life of a devoted militant was no longer for her.

She was secretly relieved at having been spared the task of proposing formation of a strike committee as

Galant had suggested she should. Marie-Claude abhorred having to speak in public.

* * *

Cheryl Keyes missed the drama of the strike at France-Dépêches, as she had a backlog of days-off earned while on assignment in Africa which she needed to take immediately. She badly needed the rest too.

Cheryl had been back in Paris less than a week when, after vomiting two more mornings in a row, she suspected she might be pregnant. This would not have been surprising, as she had flown out to Africa without renewing her contraceptive pill supply. Neither she nor Otto had taken any precautions; they had made love in Nairobi like Adam and Eve did before the serpent intervened.

A do-it-yourself urine test followed by a visit to a gynaecologist confirmed her suspicions. The doctor told her that it was too early to be sure at this stage, but that she was "possibly" pregnant with twins.

Now Cheryl was, when it came down to it, a level-headed young woman. She therefore resolved to do nothing and to say nothing to anyone about the matter until she had reflected some upon it. But she was worried alright!

* * *

For Christophe Juliet, the exit from France-Dépêches was inglorious, if not ignominious. By midday on the Sunday, barely hours after the successful strike against his plans for the agency, Juliet had begun vacating his penthouse office. He and a couple of his minions were seen carrying cartons out of the special lift that directly served the sixth-floor office.

Along with Juliet disappeared the director of public relations he had appointed, and whose utility had escaped everyone else at the agency, as well as his private personal secretary and a number of other hangers-on whose exact role or function had remained obscure.

It was only a few days later that it became clear just how much this *coterie* had been paying itself out of the agency's seriously limited funds.

There was a moment of new drama when the size of the financial hole that Juliet and his *clique* left in the accounts became known. They had somehow managed to pay themselves some handsome 'goodbye' money before getting away, it seemed.

However, the general feeling was that even at that price it was a case of good riddance of bad rubbish, seen against the certain damage that Juliet's 'action plan' would have caused to the agency and its staff.

Tensions abated considerably within France-Dépêches, and notably at its Paris headquarters, with the withdrawal of the plan and the departure of its unloved author.

But Francis Renaulde had been right to stress to the trade unions the importance of the confidence of the agency's clients. There had been slippage. Notably over the 'mystery disease' story, then on the unfolding revolution in Santa de Costa.

An important US daily paper client and a Southeast Asian press and broadcasting group had both strongly hinted that their contracts with France-Dépêches for the English-language world news-wire would be in the balance when they came up for annual renewal.

The fact was that the agency had also been under growing competitive pressure with the expansion in recent years of the Internet, which had made available to all and sundry a whole range of more-or-less free news media resources through just a couple of mouse clicks.

It mattered little to the people in the marketing and accounts departments that much of the so-called news to be gleaned on the Internet was of doubtful provenance and veracity. What did they know or care about reliable sources? And how could a casual reader of such 'news' be expected to discern the wheat from the chaff?

* * *

For Jean-François Cardenal in Santa de Costa, times were bleak. In the space of just a few days, he had learned that his wife Constanza was having an affair with the Argentine military attaché and had to confront what he considered an exorbitant salary demand by the bureau's local-hire staff, both journalists and technicians.

Cardenal was mortified at being cuckolded by a man who had been a frequent dinner party guest at his home. While politically conservative himself, he had always considered Raoûl Whateverhisnamewas to be an arrogant jack-booted semi-fascist.

As for the demands of the local staff for a 25% raise, they were in truth very moderate given the rate of inflation and the general climate of revolutionary agitation in the country, which had begun to exasperate Cardenal.

On top of which, he was expecting any day now to be recalled from his prestigious and once so pleasant posting.

* * *

In Nairobi, Andy Mitchell was enjoying a felicitous love-affair with the pretty young Njoki. His sex-life had improved radically, quality-wise. And he was also drinking much less.

These positive developments helped him stand up to the odious Bertrand Rainier who, in the absence of Henri Laborie, on annual leave after a three-day sojourn in the Omarou archipelago for a follow-up reportage on the 'mystery disease', was victimising Andy.

It seemed that Rainier suspected Andy of somehow

undermining the bureau chief's authority during the latter's bout of malaria. Possibly this was connected with the fact that unlike the bureau chief, Andy treated the local-hire black staff as human equals.

Andy had been a little taken aback on learning that Njoki was only just twenty-one years old, against his own thirty-three years, but told himself that so long as they got on well together this did not really matter.

He continued to be amazed that such a modest-seeming and sweet young girl was capable of such frank sexual ardour in the bedroom when she stayed overnight with him at Westlands.

He was truly transported as he watched her slip out of her clothes, undo her plaits, shake out her magnificent head of glistening black hair, and then lie back to receive him. Her splendidly coquettish invitation made him nearly delirious with delight.

Once inside her, he would stay there, unmoving, for as long as they both could bear it, and just weep for joy. It was like an amazing home-coming, after so much loveless coupling. He could barely believe that he was now happily fucking the little soul-mate that he had never ever dared hope to find or know.

For all of this, for her amazingly natural and girlish kindness towards him, Andy felt deeply grateful. He was thus more than ready to overlook her rather silly squeaky voice and slightly dumpy figure. He knew that she had him well and truly hooked.

CHAPTER 25

Staff at France-Dépêches had little time to savour their success in staving off the government-inspired plan which many of them had feared would all but destroy the agency and put numbers of them out of work. The never-ending succession of news soon refocussed the attention of most of its journalists.

The flow of political and economic upheavals, sporting events, wars and natural disasters, plane and train crashes, *coups d'état*, elections and revolutions, fashion and film news, stock and commodity market movements, or shipping news, is inexorable, and all of it is grist to the mill of an international news agency.

It all has to be written, rewritten, distributed and redistributed, edited, packaged and presented, doubled-checked or discarded for the agency's myriad clients and readers around the world.

After the crisis and related setbacks at France-Dépêches, the agency's management and senior editors were keen to restore its competitive edge.

* * *

Cheryl Keyes, of course, had other preoccupations. After a day's concentrated thinking about her pregnancy and Otto and general predicament, she decided that whatever her parents, Otto or anyone else thought about it, she would have the baby (or babies!).

She knew enough about the abortions of other young women in her situation to know that this was a sad and bitter experience she wanted to avoid, even if it meant interrupting her professional career and facing great social and economic uncertainties.

She thought first of writing to Otto in Dakar. She had been intending to do so anyway. But then decided to telephone him, knowing that the post would take more days than she was prepared to wait to know his views on the matter. Phone connections between Paris and the Senegalese capital were not bad.

Cheryl chose to phone Otto at this home the following morning, which was a Sunday. They had not communicated since separating in Nairobi nearly a week earlier.

When she heard his voice answering *"Allo, oui"* sleepily, and with a strong echo as if he was in the bathroom, she was undecided whether to speak in French or English. She opted for both, repeating her brief message first in English and then in French.

"Hallo, Otto, how are you doing?" she began woodenly.

"Fine. And how about you, my American beauty?"

Cheryl had at least once before explained to Otto that

'American' used in this way tended to mean 'of the United States' whereas she was Canadian and proud of it. But this was not the moment…

"Well, listen Otto. I'm fine. Only thing is, I am pregnant. *Je suis enceinte, tu m'entends?*"

"*Oui, je t'entends.*"

"What are we going to do?"

"What do you want to do?"

"I want to have it, or them. Oh, Otto, the doctor said it might be twins!"

She heard the tension in her own voice rise and felt a few hot tears spill down her cheeks.

"Cheryl, you know that I am already a father. I have to reflect about this. I will call you tonight."

Cheryl could no longer contain herself and let out a loud sob before crying into the phone: "Oh, Otto, I love you!"

"Cheryl, I love you too. But I have to think."

This was the first time they had exchanged professions of love. Although they had already promised to stay in touch, until now they had skirted around the notion of serious commitment to each other in a relationship. New circumstances added new weight to the question.

They left it there until later that evening. Meanwhile, Cheryl did some more thinking.

CHAPTER 26

In Santa de Costa, where the revolution progressed by fits and starts, the word on the local grapevine that his beautiful wife was having an affair with the Argentine military attaché all but destroyed Jean-François Cardenal's remaining self-respect.

He resigned himself to being recalled to France and put in charge of some provincial bureau and could not imagine that Constanza would follow him. As the only child of her wealthy banker father, she certainly had no need of his agency salary.

The rumour in Paris was that the director of news would be named head of the Santa de Costa bureau to replace him. In fact, however, despite the persistence of the rumour, both Cardenal and the director of news continued in their respective posts for many months more.

But these were terrible times for Jean-François Cardenal, out of step with the epoch, out of his depth, lonely and betrayed. He was fortunate that between them Grangier, the local hires and Peter Morel were able to run the bureau in Santa de Costa City without his help.

Sorry for himself, he had for the first time in his life taken to drink, tippling beyond moderation in the solitude of his palatial residence. Constanza had taken to sleeping out at night without warning, and if it had not been for the faithful housemaid Maria, he would have gone without any dinner most nights.

In so far as he could, given his professional position, Cardenal now avoided social occasions as he waited for the axe to fall.

Francis Renaulde was uncertain about how long he himself could expect to remain in the post of managing director and chief executive, given that he had replaced Juliet at such short notice and enjoyed no real support or respect in government circles, where his undeniable professional qualities counted for little.

He therefore preferred to keep the reliable and competent director of news as his right-hand man in Paris.

Not until several weeks after the crisis in the agency was Renaulde confirmed in the post of managing director and chief executive by the government and the board of directors, despite the obvious need to rapidly restore some serenity to France-Dépêches.

Philosophical and prudent, Renaulde thereafter contented himself with managing the agency from day to day.

Gareth Galant and Marie-Claude Schroedinger built a love-nest for themselves and the white long-haired cat Pitchoune in a two-room mansard apartment in Paris in the 9th *arrondissement* and continued their militant struggle in what was now to be called the Workers Party.

The party believed that France was possibly heading for a general strike very soon and was doing what it could to fulfil this prediction. There was indeed a perceptible worsening of the general political climate in the country, as the government concentrated its attacks on public sector workers and the public services, most notably in education and broadcasting.

After some two years in office, and a zealous application of European Union principles in favour of unfettered free enterprise and budget cuts, the administration was a darling of the financial sector but at an all-time low in the public opinion polls.

Fully recovered from his cardiac alert, Galant was torn between his professional career and his political and trade union commitments. He was in line for the job of national secretary of the Democratic Union of Journalists, or he could apply for a post in the agency as a service or bureau chief. Meanwhile, he was having to deal with his wife's divorce action. She had hired an expensive lawyer with the evident aim of suing him for all the money and property that she could.

Ventrex, for his part, was repeatedly said to be in line for the post of director of news which he had long coveted. But in the absence of the long-rumoured rotation of posts, he accepted the prestigious position of chief of the London bureau of France-Dépêches. It was rumoured that the prime minister had personally vetoed him for the top journalistic job at the agency.

With the immediate crisis in the agency over, Ventrex virtually ceased all trade union activity.

In Nairobi, Henri Laborie agreed to fill a newly-created post of deputy regional director under Rainier, although he had been seeking a Middle East posting. Andy was only slightly put out by this. He would have liked to be asked but would not have wanted the responsibility of even being deputy bureau chief. It was enough for him that Njoki had been hinting heavily that she would like them to get married!

Andy, who had several weeks of leave owing to him before he would be obliged to return to Europe – if he was to stay with the agency – was still considering possible career moves in the light of his relationship with Njoki.

Rainier was a few months later named chief of the Moscow bureau, despite his almost total ignorance of the Russian language and Russian affairs. His odious behaviour and pathological paranoia soon had the whole Moscow bureau up in arms against him.

Not the least of Francis Renaulde's difficulties in the top job was how to deal with a virtual ultimatum from the Moscow bureau staff to the effect: "Either Rainier goes, or we do."

The dilemma was resolved by recalling Rainier after less than a year in Moscow while offering him the job of chief defence affairs correspondent for the agency, a post which accorded perfectly with the man's obsessive military fantasies.

Another difficulty was what to do with Jean-François Cardenal. He was given leave of absence to help him 'dry out' at a clinic where they were used to treating journalists, actors, musicians and so forth, before being named to head the bureau of Limoges – exactly the kind of backwater he'd been so apprehensive of.

Constanza had indeed left him, though whether for the Argentine military attaché Raoûl Whatshisname or not Jean-François neither knew nor cared any longer. He was now on the look-out for a suitably homely French woman.

As for the man who had caused all the recent trouble, Christophe Juliet, he was last heard of offering 'consultant services' to Internet companies wanting to break into the news distribution business. He remained apparently undaunted, confident even in his abilities and prospects, and was above all still wealthy.

Meanwhile, some said the agency was now just drifting along in a state of suspended animation until the next inevitable crisis came.

As for the 'viral plague', it all but petered out as mysteriously as it had erupted. Minor, isolated new outbreaks were occasionally reported, but VAP1, as it had come to be officially known (standing for Viral African

Plague One), joined a host of other unpleasant infectious diseases that inhabitants of the so-called dark continent have to contend with.

CHAPTER 27

Intrepid as well as brave, in the weeks following confirmation of her pregnancy and her decision to see it through, Cheryl artfully persuaded Otto to quit Africa and settle in Paris with her, at least until the babies were born. He was, she realised, proud to have an attractive white woman for a mistress and to have made her pregnant.

She convinced him that until the birth her salary could – just about – keep the two of them, and explained to him that in any event, France-Dépêches was obliged to take her back after her maternity leave. Cheryl had begun to understand the value of the collective social rights won by workers in France.

She also persuaded her parents, once they had recovered from the first shock of her situation, to help the couple secure a modest three-room apartment in the 11th *arrondissement* while waiting for their twins to be born. Otto, meanwhile, hoped to work as a freelance (or stringer) in Paris for PANA and for both West African and East African newspapers.

Cheryl, for a time, had a fixation with going to settle in Sweden with Otto and the forthcoming babies, persuaded that a mixed-race couple would suffer the least prejudice there. She even contacted Bengt Danielssen in Nairobi – the man who first introduced Cheryl and Otto to each other – about a job in Sweden.

However, Otto feared the cold Scandinavian climate, and he wanted them to move to the United States. But immigration difficulties for Otto – and the fact that they were not married, for he still had a legal wife in Gulu, Uganda, under local traditional law – made them also consider Canada.

Nine months after their first night together in Nairobi's River Road, Cheryl gave birth to twin boys. To Otto's initial dismay, as this made for a rather cramped apartment, Cheryl's mother flew over to Paris from Montreal to be with her daughter at this time.

But he soon appreciated Mrs Keyes' presence – not least because she cooked for them all and took the immediate pressure of parenthood off him. This allowed Otto to concentrate on the little journalistic work he has able to find – and which soon proved inadequate from the point of view of the remuneration it brought.

Proud, aristocratic even, in his outlook and attitudes, Otto was nevertheless obliged to find other, more menial work. Having entered France on a tourist visa, he was not legally allowed to work, but thanks to friends in Dakar, Senegal, found casual part-time work in an African restaurant in the quarter of Barbès.

After a month with Cheryl, Otto and the twins, Mrs Keyes returned to Canada, leaving the couple and their offspring to their own devices. They settled into a life of young family domesticity, occasionally entertaining friends and colleagues of each of them to dinner, or dining with friends and colleagues, when not absorbed by professional work or childcare.

Somewhat unexpectedly, Otto also developed into something of a computer geek, establishing a minor side-line in the construction and repair of cheap PCs for African and Arab clients whom he met through his work in the Senegalese restaurant.

The next big change for Cheryl and Otto came after Cheryl returned to work – part-time at first – on the English desk in Paris, when the twins were six months old. Cheryl had already decided that she wanted a posting in Africa and let this be known among her immediate colleagues and the agency hierarchy, for discreet lobbying was generally considered an essential way of getting where and what you wanted in France-Dépêches.

She thus duly applied for and won the job of staff anglophone correspondent in Johannesburg, despite sharp competition for the post.

Before taking up the South African posting, Cheryl decided to make a visit to Montreal with the twins to present them to both her parents.

Otto thereupon decided to visit his wife and ten-year-old daughter in Gulu, Uganda, both to provide them with some funds and also to seek a divorce – or at least make it clear to the unfortunate woman that he was leaving her for good.

He and Cheryl agreed to meet up again in Johannesburg for their new life there after their respective trips on personal business.

In Gulu, village neighbours told Otto his wife had paid a witchdoctor to put a spell on him, to make him come back to her, failing which he would fall sick and infect his new wife.

When he made clear to his wife that he was leaving her for good, they had a fearful row, in the course of which she swung at his head with a *panga* (machete) that she had evidently been keeping handy for such a purpose.

Fortunately, the *panga* was blunt as well as rusty, but he nevertheless suffered an ugly wound and severe bruising on the left side of his neck. Otto had some difficulty in explaining this injury to inquirers over the following days and weeks.

PART TWO

PART TWO

CHAPTER 28

By the time Andy Mitchell reached the scene, the police photographers and forensic scientists had already left. The pavement was being hosed clean of blood and bits of brain, and the body of the victim had been loaded into a police van, blue lights flashing and siren wailing, to be taken away for safekeeping in a Marseilles mortuary.

The scene was still gruesome enough for Andy, however.

The victim was André Santoni, brother of the senator and former Marseilles mayor Gérard Santoni. It was Gérard Santoni who would be asked to formally identify the body, a challenging task given that half of the head had been ripped away by a volley of heavy-calibre automatic weapon fire.

Of Corsican descent, the Santoni family were prominent in Marseilles. Gérard Santoni, the elder of the two, was a local leader of France's main right-wing party, the Union of French Citizens (UFC) and a property landlord with interests in construction. The unfortunate André owned several bars and a nightclub.

Two men on a motorcycle had forced his car to a halt, pulled him out from the back seat and shot him at point-blank range – the pillion passenger wielding what appeared to be a large assault rifle – before speeding away, according to André Santoni's driver, who was the only witness. The shock of the killing had reduced him to a gibbering wreck.

Andy had been paying a routine morning news-gathering visit to the Marseilles bureau of France-Dépêches when the latter received a tip from a confidential police source of a gang-style killing in one of the notoriously violent northern quarters of the Mediterranean port city, and he had decided to accompany the agency staff reporter and a photographer to the scene.

Crime reporting was not something that Andy had done much of since his cub reporter days in Britain. But in the few months he had been free-lancing in the Marseilles region, he had needed to turn his hand to all kinds of journalism. Moreover, this was no small-time affair, and came on top of other recent gangland killings in the city.

He decided to work up a story on organised crime in Marseilles around the killing that he could offer to a British tabloid. It would make a change from some of the drudge work he had been doing lately on shipping and industry for trade papers and magazines. As a former staff journalist of France-Dépêches, the bureau would let him use their archives.

It was now more than a year since Andy had left Kenya and his staff job at France-Dépêches. He and Njoki had married in a civil ceremony at the attorney-general's office in Nairobi before the two of them headed for Europe and a new life together. His workmate at the Nairobi bureau, Henri Laborie, had been his witness at the ceremony. Njoki's witness had been her flatmate Irene, the leggy Kamba girl.

Unable to face the prospect of going back to the news desk in Paris with the end of his posting to East Africa, Andy had decided to try his hand at free-lancing out of Marseilles, acting on the theory that there would be little competition from other anglophone journalists in that city, though in practice it had been proving very hard to find enough work.

He had also quite rightly surmised that Njoki would prefer Marseilles to Paris, not least because the weather was much warmer, but also because of its multi-cultural melting-pot aspect. Njoki loved the city even more than he did. "It's just like Mombasa," she squeaked delightedly on their first day.

Njoki was taking classes in French during much of the day but ensured that Andy had a good square meal waiting when he came home of an evening to their tiny studio flat near the old waterfront. She was hoping to get work in a bank when her French was good enough.

Not long after arriving in Marseilles, Andy had been upset to learn the fate of Cairo-based France-Dépêches photographer Ali Younis Ghotbadzeh and another agency journalist. Younis, as he was generally known, had lost a foot, blown off at the ankle in an explosion when the vehicle he was riding in apparently hit a landmine in the Sinai desert, according to what Andy learned from colleagues in the Marseilles bureau.

Younis, who was of both Arab and Persian extraction, had been on a trip to the Sinai with a French reporter recently recruited to the agency's Cairo bureau as a local hire, Jean Millon, who was killed outright in the incident. Two other reporters, one from a Belgian newspaper, the other working for Netherlands state radio, escaped with severe shock, cuts and bruises. The Bedouin driver of their Toyota Landcruiser was badly wounded.

The party had been investigating the situation in the Sinai in the wake of the revolution in Egypt which had seen the overthrow of President Hosni Mubarak. All sorts of violent clashes between Egyptian paramilitary police forces and unidentified other armed groups had been repeatedly reported in the vast desert territory in recent weeks, and the zone was officially strictly out of bounds. With the eruption of the revolution which drove President Mubarak from power, the Cairo bureau had become especially busy.

The party of journalists had been on the second day of their excursion into the Sinai when the incident occurred, and the details were not clear. They had gone into the region precisely because the situation on the ground there had become especially obscure due to the activities of various armed groups.

A military police helicopter evacuated the casualties to a Cairo military hospital, and the deputy head of France-Dépêches personnel, Marie-France Perrault, flew out to Cairo to see what the agency could do for Younis, one of its star photographers. Younis had won several awards for his battle-zone pictures, most notably in Iraq during the second Gulf War.

Although the Landcruiser was blown up 'accidentally' by a landmine, according to the official account of the Egyptian police patrol unit first on the scene, there was a suspicion among the Cairo press corps that it had been a deliberate ambush.

Andy had a fond recollection of Younis as a jovial genius organiser of parties with dancing girls and free-flowing liquor for the two memorable weeks that they had shared a villa in Mogadishu, the divided and battle-torn capital of Somalia. This despite a strict curfew and the pervading Islamic puritanism that had taken hold in Somalia as elsewhere in the Middle East and the Horn of Africa.

In an earlier life, Younis had been an active member of the *mujahideen* (Islamic combatants) during the Islamic Revolution in Iran. Andy remembered him for his courage as well as his unfailing good humour, and wondered if this injury meant the complete end of the photographer's professional career. In any event, he expected that Younis would be properly compensated and cared for by the agency. So far as Andy could recall, Younis had a wife and family in the port town of Basrah.

* * *

Police investigations into the assassination of André Santoni apparently went nowhere, just like those into previous but less spectacular recent killings. The government promised police reinforcements for Marseilles in the face of anguished hand-wringing on the part of local elected officials concerned at the notoriety that the city was earning.

But nothing seemed really to change, and no-one knew or was saying what the killings were about. As usual, the French media simply attributed them to *'règlements de compte'* (settling of scores) between gangsters, which wasn't saying much.

A flourishing local drugs trade, 'turf wars', so-called vice-rings and protection rackets, conflicts over construction contracts – you could take your pick. But such stories lacked the strong sources that Andy, as a former agency reporter, was used to quoting in his articles.

Despite trying to further exploit the Marseilles crime scene for its apparently spicy news value, Andy found that he could get a clearer handle on stories related to the shipping industry, for example. He thus cultivated contacts with trade union officials fighting the closure of the port's repair dockyards, or in conflict over its important ferry services and container traffic.

He was not about to become a police reporter again,

he decided. Yet on the other hand, Andy also knew that violent crime generally made for more eye-grabbing headlines than 'social conflict'. 'If it bleeds, it leads', was a tried-and-tested, if somewhat cynical, adage of the hack's trade. And basically, if you are a reporter, you know that 'news is news' whatever the subject matter.

CHAPTER 29

Within France-Dépêches, more than a year-and-a-half after the crisis that saw the resignation of the government's choice of managing director in the face of trade union resistance to his job cuts and privatisation plan, the situation had long since returned to normal. Apparently, at least.

After a few uncertain weeks as interim manging director, Francis Renaulde was confirmed in the post and contented himself with expediting current affairs. That is, he ensured the day-to-day running of a complex, specialised organisation which relied on the skill and devotion of its staff, above all the journalists, of which he was definitely one – unlike his unlamented predecessor.

And indeed things continued upon a relatively uneventful course at the agency, if not in the world at large, for the next few months or so.

Then came the day that Andy Mitchell received a call from Gareth Galant, reminding him of his political duties as a paid-up member of the Workers Party and militant of the journalists' section of the Democratic Union.

Galant suggested to Andy that they needed to talk, and asked Andy if he might be planning a trip to Paris in the near future. Warming instantly to the idea, Andy decided to combine overdue medical appointments with a long weekend in Paris to see Galant and other old friends and colleagues.

Andy suddenly realised that he was pleased of the change of scene that the trip would mean. It would also mean finally getting his eyes tested and having his liver checked out. Ever since a bout of hepatitis contracted in Addis Ababa, Andy had worried about his liver – though not to the extent of giving up all alcohol, far from it!

Njoki was displeased to learn that Andy was planning a few days in Paris without her, but had no choice in the matter.

* * *

Andy and Gareth Galant had lunch in a restaurant not far from the France-Dépêches head office, called Les Falaises du Cap, in the Rue Montorgueil. Andy knew the street and its open market well for having sold the party newspaper there on Sunday mornings before he went to Africa.

Gareth had already intimated to Andy that he would like the Englishman to return to the agency: to help strengthen the journalists' section of the Democratic Union, of course, but above all to resume activity in the Workers Party cell within the agency.

"Sooner or later – probably sooner – there's going to be another crisis at France-Dépêches and so I want to be able to rely on you.

"You've had your years in Africa, you're now a married man back in France and we need you. There's no longer any good reason for you not to take part in union and party politics at the agency. As you know, with full staff status you would be well-protected, unlike a freelance or a correspondent far away in the field."

For Andy, the political and trade union side of things posed no problem – he had after all remained a paid-up member of both organisations throughout his posting in Nairobi, even though he had, for practical and security reasons, renounced all open militant activity during his time in Africa.

Galant wanted Andy in a staff-status job in Paris. However, Andy did not want to leave Marseilles for Paris, and knew well that Njoki wouldn't want to move either.

"How about if I returned to the agency but stayed in Marseilles as an English-language correspondent?" he asked Galant. The fact was that it would suit Andy economically to be back on a regular salary.

"That would mean a job creation if it was a full staff-status posting," Galant pointed out, as if Andy did not already realise this. "I don't think management would wear that, in the present climate, even if it can theoretically be justified. They might accept a local-hire posting, but then I don't think the unions would. I know that we in the Democratic Union wouldn't."

Galant paused to let his words sink in.

"Let me sound out the various parties. You could also check out the question with the English desk in Paris. After all, it's them that you would be working for, and you've already got some friends there." *Yes, and a few enemies*, Andy thought to himself.

Their conversation turned to the general political situation in France, which had undergone considerable upheavals in recent weeks. In short, the radical right-wing government that had been causing such unrest among the country's workforce over the last three years or so was no longer in office.

The all-out general strike long predicted by the Workers Party never quite happened – division among the leaders of the various trade union confederations had ensured that. The change was, above all, due to the fact that the government decided to call a snap general election in a bid to head off the unrest, and had then, to widespread surprise, narrowly lost that election.

The Socialist Party was back in power, with the participation of the ecologist Greens Party and what remained of the once-powerful Communist Party – albeit with an uncomfortably narrow majority in parliament.

The situation appeared as unstable as ever, and none of the parties to the new equation found cause for satisfaction. But for the powers-that-be, the political and economic establishment, the change of government at least meant a breathing space.

Politics was not what Andy Mitchell had on his mind at this particular moment, however. From the time they had entered the restaurant, he had been fascinated by the waitress who served the two of them. The instant he saw her, he desired her fiercely. And each time he looked at her, that desire gripped him.

He felt embarrassed and ashamed that he should once again be experiencing one of his mad moments of wild, unsatisfied and apparently irrational sexual desire, despite the fact of his being happily married to Njoki. Was he perhaps not so happily married after all? He had obscurely imagined such moments behind him and was thus caught off-guard.

The fact of the matter – if one could speak of fact in such a context – was that this woman was, for him, delightfully, deliciously, extraordinarily and unusually beautiful. Her desirability struck him like a surprise blow to the solar plexus. She made him want to cry out with a wondrous, desperate pain.

You fool! he silently admonished himself. *You're still falling in love with waitresses like the adolescent you'll always stay!* And yet at the same time, he experienced a strange strong sensation that these thoughts and feelings were the confirmation of an ancient truth.

She was blonde, sharp-featured, with a pointed angular jaw, a large mouth full of bright white teeth, and huge liquid-green eyes. She was probably as tall as he was, but very slim, almost anorexically so: flat-chested, bony-hipped. As his brain whirled, all he could think was that she was 'to die for' and cursed himself for an idiot.

"*Je vois qu'elle te plaît,*" (I can see you fancy her) Galant remarked.

"*Heh, oui!*" Andy confirmed.

Long after they had finished their meal, paid and left, his mind kept returning to the waitress, making him breathless with renewed surges of unhappy desire.

CHAPTER 30

Andy knew full well that it was folly to seek to embark upon any kind of sexual adventure with the waitress, but knew equally well that he was bound to try his luck. And so he returned to the restaurant that evening in order to see her again and try to seduce her.

She was there alright, and every bit as desirable as he had been imagining all afternoon. She recognised him, eyebrows raised in surprise at his return, but gave him what he chose to interpret as an encouraging smile. He ordered a salad this time, as his lunch had been copious, and asked to know her name.

"*Je m'appelle Stéphanie.*"

"*Moi, c'est Andrew.*"

He obviously couldn't know how it sounded to her, but to himself it sounded odd, this 'Andrew'. Everyone for years now only called him Andy.

"*Est-ce que je peux t'attendre jusqu'à la fin de ton service ?*" (Can I wait for you until the end of your shift?) he asked.

"*Si tu veux.*" (If you like)

They were already on familiar terms then, using the

'*tu*' and '*toi*' form, despite being strangers to one another. At lunch they had used the '*vous*' form as befits the relation between customer and waiter or waitress in a restaurant.

So he waited until she had finished her shift, having left an over-generous tip on the table. As the restaurant was now closing and she had a few final tasks to perform, he offered to wait outside for her.

"*Si tu veux.*" (If you like)

She looked him in the eye, and he felt himself gasp inwardly. He was unable to gauge her expression or the tone of her voice. As he stared back at her he thought he detected a slight divergent strabismus, which made eye contact with her seem hazardous – and dangerously exciting.

"*Puis-je vous accompagner ?*" (May I accompany you?) he asked, his instinct leading him to use the polite form again, and forgetting in that instant that they were already on familiar terms.

"*Mais qu'est-ce que tu veux ?*" (But what do you want?)

"*Je veux faire l'amour avec toi !*" (I want to make love with you!) he replied, hoping that his voice betrayed no tremor.

"*C'est vrai ? Allons-y donc !*" (Really? Let's go then!)
"*T'es toujours aussi téméraire avec les filles ?*" (Are you always so forward with the girls?)

"*Pas toujours,*" (Not always) he laughed nervously.

She explained that she normally took a taxi home after working late at the restaurant; her boss paid for it. But if he wanted to pay for the taxi and give her the receipt, he could. That way she could save the taxi allowance for herself.

She lived in the 17th *arrondissement,* in a modern block of what are described by estate agents as luxury flats. The apartment was expensively furnished, but in a neutral style.

She offered him a cognac and poured one for herself. From the kitchen she led him to the salon and pointed to a divan but sat herself down in an armchair and took off her shoes.

"*Tu es marié ?*" (Are you married?) she asked him.

"*Oui,*" he admitted grudgingly.

"*Je m'en doutais.*" (I guessed so.)

"*Et toi?*"

"*J'ai un fiancé. Il est banquier. C'est lui qui m'a trouvé cet appart'. Il est vraiment très gentil.*" (I have a fiancé. He's a banker. He found me this flat. He's really very kind.)

Andy imagined a gentleman of a certain age but abstained from comment.

He felt a little awkward and was wondering how to advance; the ambiance was cold, if not clinical. But she took the initiative.

"*On y va alors ? Allons au lit donc !*" (Shall we get to it then? Let's go to bed.)

She began undressing on her way to what was evidently the bedroom, leaving Andy to follow her and follow suit.

In the stark halogen light of a bedside lamp, he was able to briefly admire her tall, extraordinarily slim, pale body; utterly flat-chested and more achingly beautiful than anything he could have imagined, before she threw herself onto the bed and wrapped herself tightly in the bedclothes.

Suddenly he felt painfully lost and alone, unable to bridge the gulf he sensed between them with any gesture of love, affection or desire. *Yet another gross error of judgement in my relations with others,* he cursed bitterly to himself.

* * *

He woke unusually early the next morning. It seemed to be still dark both inside the apartment and outside, though he could already hear the clamour of the city: delivery vans, garbage trucks, he guessed; then a distant siren…

Jumping up from the bed, he hunted around for his

clothes and hurriedly dressed, ill at ease and eager to be on his way. As he stumbled toward the door, he heard her move and felt guilty that he had been planning to steal away without a word.

He stepped back to the bed and bent to kiss her, but she moved away from him. He had the feeling she did not recognise him at all, had no recollection of their short night together. Indeed, he hoped she did not remember. She said not a word and nor did he.

In the hallway of the apartment he found a light switch and actioned it. In the dim light he saw himself reflected in the sickly yellow of a large mirror and quickly averted his gaze. From his wallet he took a 50-euro note, two twenties and a ten and placed them on top of what looked like some bills and junk mail on a small table by the entry door of the flat.

Andy knew then that he would be unable to return to that restaurant for fear of seeing her again, for shame. It had not been a very good night for either of them.

Meeting the light of day on the street outside, in a quarter of Paris that was unfamiliar to him, which felt hostile even, he felt a pang of desire for the company of Njoki, cherishing in his mind her kindness, her receptivity and her tightly-rounded buttocks. How many times had he told her: *"Ton cul est mon salut"* (Your arse is my salvation) ?

CHAPTER 31

Cheryl Keyes and her Otto had by now been living for a few months in the multi-cultural Hillbrow district of Johannesburg with their twin boys, whom they had named Lucas and Leon.

Cheryl was kept very busy by her work in the Jo'burg bureau because South Africa generated a regular flow of news, even if much of it was of regional or 'third-world' interest rather than 'world news'.

This meant that Otto found himself in the role of 'house-husband', looking after the twins, notwithstanding the full-time, live-in maid-cum-nanny that they had inherited from another France-Dépêches correspondent after the latter's posting to the bureau came to an end.

What freelance work he was able to do for PANA and regional African newspapers neither kept him fully occupied nor paid very much.

But they had settled into the life of a stable married couple – even if Otto had been unable yet to disentangle himself from his wife and child back in Uganda. He regularly sent them a bit of money and tried to do so out of his own pocket rather than Cheryl's salary.

They had a full social life among the international community in Johannesburg.

And for the first time in her adult life, Cheryl succeeded in losing quite a few pounds of excess weight, without soon gaining them again. The change suited her admirably; now she really came across as a breath-taking blonde bombshell. Her looks and natural charm were more advantageous than ever for her, professionally and personally.

* * *

The steady worsening of the situation in South Africa, marked by deepening corruption, overt political dissent and division, continued violent crime and a general sharpening of the class struggle, ensured that there was plenty to write about.

The 'honey-moon' period of Nelson Mandela's presidency was by now long past. Indeed, it seemed that the material and moral situation of the black majority was for the most part worse than ever, despite the formal end of apartheid.

Then came the Marikana massacre in 2012, and things would never be the same in post-apartheid South Africa, or Azania, as political militants of the black majority call it.

Here's a report of the Marikana massacre as provided by France-Dépêches, which unfortunately failed to excel in getting this prime piece of news out fast enough or to express it in appropriately sharp prose, creditable though the bureau's efforts no doubt were. But let the reader judge:

More than 30 dead in police clash with striking South African miners

JOHANNESBURG, 17 August – More than 30 miners on strike at a South African platinum mine were killed Thursday in a clash with police amid rivalry among competing trade unions, the police ministry said.

The leader of the more militant miners' union accused management of the Lonmin mine of colluding with a rival union to produce the massacre, in what was the country's deadliest day of protest since the end of apartheid in the early 1990s.

National television showed riot police wearing body armour shooting at workers amid scenes of panic and confusion that left numerous bodies on the ground amid pools of blood.

South African President Jacob Zuma condemned the killings but made no reference to the handling of the situation by the police. "We are shocked and dismayed at this senseless violence," he said.

The deaths came after a week of turmoil at the Marikana mine that had already seen 10 people killed, including two police officers and two security guards.

Lonmin, the world's third biggest platinum producer, has suspended production at the mine, about 60 miles (95 kilometres) north-west of Johannesburg, after what it called an illegal strike escalated into a turf war between rival unions.

His voice shaking with anger, Joseph Mathunjwa, president of the breakaway Association of Mineworkers and Construction Union (AMCU), accused Lonmin management of colluding with the National Union of Mineworkers (NUM).

The NUM denied collusion with mine bosses and accused the AMCU of poaching its members in South Africa's important mining industry.

The protests began when mineworkers demanded a pay increase to 12,500 rand (about 500 dollars US) a month.

Helen Zille, leader of the opposition Democratic Alliance, called for an independent investigation to determine the cause of the violence.

The alleged massacre comes amid growing frustration with the governing African National Congress (ANC) and its mainstream trade union allies for moving too slowly to deliver wage increases and public services.

South Africa is home to four-fifths of the world's known platinum reserves but has been hit by union militancy and a sharp drop in the price of the precious metal this year.

Lonmin chairman Roger Phillimore said in a written statement: "The South African police service have been in charge of public order and safety on the ground since the violence between competing labour factions erupted over the weekend, claiming the lives of eight of our employees and two police officers.

"It goes without saying that we deeply regret the further loss of life in what is clearly a public order rather than labour relations-associated matter."

A spokesman at Lonmin's head office in London confirmed strikers had been served with an ultimatum to return to work on Thursday or face dismissal but denied this had inflamed the situation.

The company's shares fell by over 7% on the London Stock Exchange Thursday. Lonmin's South African operations, suspended since the killings, account for 12% of global platinum production.

Whether it was because the lead paragraph of the main 'write-through' or 'roundup story' lacked punch, or whether France-Dépeches had simply been too slow off the mark, the controls showed that clients subscribing to all three big main agencies had preferred to take Beckers' copy, or even that of Amalgamated Press. Of course, the true reason was hard to find, in any event, for there is always a certain element of chance in such matters.

Cheryl, for she was among those who had handled the Johannesburg copy on that fateful day in 'post-apartheid South Africa', wondered whether they should not have tried to put the event in a more historical context as of the lead paragraph, the one that is supposed to immediately grab the attention of clients and news editors.

Thus she thought, after the event, that perhaps it should have read something more like this:

More than 30 dead in police clash with striking South African miners

JOHANNESBURG, 17 August – More than 30 miners on strike at a South African platinum mine were killed Thursday in a clash with police in one of the country's bloodiest protests since the end of apartheid, officials said.

The alleged massacre at the Marikana mine came amid rivalry among competing miners' trade unions, the police ministry said.

National television showed riot police wearing body armour shooting at workers amid scenes of panic and confusion that left numerous bodies on the ground amid pools of blood...

The 'lead' of a news story, that first and preferably not-too-long sentence of a news story – or newspaper article for the layman – is, according to the craft of news agency journalists, supposed to be the one that grabs the attention of the reader, whether they be newspaper editor, radio station copy-taster or whatever kind of client.

The impact of that lead sentence indeed should,

according to a certain news agency lore, be 'like the prostitute's smile'. That is to say, seduce with promise. A 'lead' should therefore be 'sexy'. Of course, as with the prostitute's smile, the client expects the promise to be followed by a development: the story thus 'led' therefore must 'stand up' or be borne out by the subsequently aligned facts and quotations.

But these are technical considerations. The undeniable fact is that the Marikana massacre constituted and constitutes an historic turning point in the South African political and economic situation. The event demonstrated dramatically for most South Africans – the black majority – that despite the end of apartheid, political and economic emancipation was still a long way off.

Indeed, for many, the material and moral situation had even worsened since the turn of the century. In short, the African National Congress, historically the mainstream liberation movement of the country's black majority, had run its course. That was the political lesson of Marikana, as Cheryl later wrote in a 'think-piece'.

Formally, the ANC of Nelson Mandela, Oliver Tambo and Walter Sisulu took power as of 1994 following the introduction of majority rule under the Kempton Park accords.

But thereafter, the country had seen increasing inequality and corruption, to the extent that the presidency of Joseph Zuma had become a byword for corruption, with

Zuma himself its incarnation, to the lasting detriment of the ANC. It was in that context that Marikana occurred, and in that same context that Cheryl Keyes exercised her profession of journalist for France-Dépêches.

CHAPTER 32

Despite the vicissitudes of the class struggle and the toll of the months and years, the Trotskyist group within the agency was still active and animated by Gareth Galant, with Andy Mitchell still a loyal member. And as an anglophone comrade, it fell to him to contact Cheryl and suggest she take an interest in the work of the party's South African comrades.

It was thanks to this that the Johannesburg bureau of the agency gave serious coverage to a rally organised by the small but ambitious Socialist Unity Party of South Africa, and even published an interview with its president, who had once been a leader of the ANC's youth wing before breaking away in the name of political and economic independence for the country's working class and peasantry.

Cheryl's political education and professional work on the ground stood her in good stead. For the period following Marikana saw the rise of an important wave of black student protest in South Africa.

Thanks to the contacts and analyses of the local Trotskyist comrades, she was able to ensure almost single-handedly that the coverage by France-Dépêches of the student and trade union movements was exemplary and greatly appreciated by the agency's clients, near and far. Briskly and boldly factual as should be for an agency, it was quite unlike the ideological product of the local media and international competitors.

A spin-off effect of all this was that Otto too was inspired in his freelance writing upon South African events for PANA and his African newspaper clients as he emulated Cheryl's work.

* * *

For Andy too, there was no getting away from the class struggle. There was a dockers' strike in Marseilles. That meant professional work: handling the news stories that this generated. But there was also a political side for him as a paid-up member of the Workers Party, as their group was now called, such as selling the party newspaper at rallies in support of the strikers.

Gareth Galant had been unable to persuade Andy to try for a job on the English desk in Paris. Indeed, even if he had wanted one, it was by no means sure that he could have found a slot there. On the other hand, Andy was taken on as a 'stringer' in Marseilles for the English service of France-Dépêches. And that provided some basic bread-and-butter. It was certainly better than taking his chances as an irregular free-lance.

Not having staff status also meant he could still turn his hand to free-lance work for other media clients – just so long as he didn't work for the competition, Beckers and Amalgamated Press, of course.

Galant got some satisfaction from the fact that Andy – whom he had recruited during the latter's formative English desk years in Paris – was now once again an active party member who regularly took part in the fortnightly meetings of one of the Workers Party cells in Marseilles.

CHAPTER 33

Inevitably, as Gareth Galant had predicted, and after some premonitory rumblings a few short months down the line, the future of France-Dépêches appeared once more to be in the balance. The new crisis was of course again about money: not enough of it coming into the agency, and too much of it going out, especially in so far as the salaries of its journalists and other staff were concerned.

The new Socialist Party-led government, the so-called '*gauche plurielle*' coalition involving the environmentalist Greens Party, had not waited long before disappointing those of its supporters who still harboured any illusions about its nature.

Its style may have been less brash than that of its right-wing predecessor, but the content of this government's policies signalled little change. It was 'business as usual', to the extent that the new prime minister of France had, in a speech to a City of London audience of bankers, brokers and fund managers, just announced, in English, what everyone already new full well: "My government is pro-business!"

This notably meant more privatisations, as well as proposed changes in labour law and social legislation to the advantage of the employers and to the detriment of salaried workers, young people, the retired and so on.

For a few short weeks, the fact of an incoming Socialist

Party-led coalition with the minority Greens, supported by the ever-declining official Communists, had brought respite to the situation, a general easing of tensions, after the confrontations characteristic of the previous right-wing government. But it brought no real change.

And crucially for France-Dépêches, the new administration brought no increase in the direct and indirect government subsidies that ensured the agency's survival. The Socialist Party-led government was no more inclined than its right-wing conservative predecessor to fund the agency. And this led to a controversial financial rescue scheme...

Francis Renaulde had wisely chosen to take early retirement after eighteen months at the head of the agency, no doubt sensing that trouble was once again on the way and that he could no longer be sure of support in the government and among certain key media representatives on the governing council. It would thus fall to the new man (little question of a woman!) brought in at the top to find a solution.

Aided by the fact that he did at least have a press and broadcasting background, the new man, Hubert Henschel, apparently counselled by financial and property specialists linked to the government, basically proposed to mortgage the agency's purpose-built headquarters on the Place de l'Horloge, of which France-Dépêches was the sole owner.

Ostensibly not so controversial as the plan of the

unlamented former chief executive, the hope of Managing Director Henschel was to raise some twenty-five million euros in this way.

But the scheme could nevertheless be, once again, reasonably interpreted as contrary to the agency's still-unchanged founding charter. This still forbade any group or body from gaining undue influence, in that it risked placing France-Dépêches in debt to the banks or other financial institutions, who would be consenting to provide such funds in exchange for both a stake in a prime piece of central Paris real estate and a potential editorial lever.

Under Galant's leadership, the Democratic Union sections at the agency were predictably vociferous in their opposition to this new plan, painting it as highly dangerous for the independence of the agency, which no doubt it was.

However, the other trade unions, and notably the General Union, in which Paul Ventrex was still influential, regarded the plan as acceptable, on the basis that it would – theoretically, at least – have no bearing on editorial policy.

For its supporters – and notably Ventrex, who was suddenly back on the scene again at the Place de l'Horloge, notwithstanding his position as director of the London bureau – the proposed financial arrangement was 'none of the unions' business'.

This position constituted a remarkable turnabout. For years, under the leadership of Ventrex, and with

Communist Party support, the General Union had exposed itself to accusations of seeking to 'co-manage' the agency together with the official management.

Indeed, Galant had thereby made his reputation, splitting off from the General Union to join and then lead the Democratic Union, precisely by opposing Ventrex and his supporters on the grounds of their alleged 'co-management' of the agency.

With supreme irony, Ventrex and other General Union figures now accused Galant's Democratic Union of seeking to meddle in management matters which were not its concern.

It had originally been Galant's hope that he could rely on Andy being in Paris to help in the fight to stave off the plan to mortgage the agency's headquarters. In the event, when it came to another mass meeting of journalists and other staff in the main editorial room in the Place de l'Horloge to discuss the Henschel plan, Galant and the Democratic Union were defeated, and the other unions, led by the General Union, won the day, basically declaring their neutrality on the financial plan, which could now go ahead unhindered. Or so everyone thought...

Once again, government-management plans for the agency were upset, this time by a sudden nervous dip in the Paris region property market. That at least was the explanation for a subsequent failure to follow through on the Henschel plan.

Seemingly, it was suddenly realised that there was already an excess of empty office space in the capital, and so the potential investors who were going to rescue the agency – speculators, to give them their more appropriate name – suddenly had cold feet.

And so, despite its great reluctance to do so, the government of the day found itself once again forced to bail out France-Dépêches, with a long-term loan of twenty-five million euros – the exact same amount as the Henschel plan was supposed to provide – on top of the many millions the agency already owed in the public and private sector.

This new turnabout fed speculation in the specialised press that Henschel himself was now on a slippery slope and could soon be replaced. But as the weeks went by, the agency returned to its frequent, if not usual, state of torpor, its top hierarchy unchanged, as the powers-that-be in the Elysée and Matignon palaces and the finance ministry evidently had other fish to fry.

And so the French news agency carried on much as before, dealing with the daily news, big and small, until…

CHAPTER 34

Unannounced, a gigantic tidal wave, caused by a hugely powerful undersea earthquake located in the southern hemisphere between Australia and East Timor, swept over a large part of south-east Asia.

Before even the geophysical observatories issued their seismic reports, France-Dépêches staff on duty in Paris and elsewhere received the first news of the tsunami when they read it on their own news-wires, just seconds after it was reported by the agency's Sydney bureau via Hong Kong.

Now for France-Dépêches, as for its rivals, Hong Kong is more than just a big regional bureau. Like Paris and Washington, the special Chinese territory is also home to a regional agency news desk, that is, it is a news treatment centre, not only receiving the news from regional correspondents, but also from all other bureaux on the Asian continent, which is then edited in Hong Kong before being sent out to regional clients and the rest of the agency's world network.

Recognising the importance of the news of the tsunami, the France-Dépêches editors on duty in Hong Kong sent the first reports out for urgent immediate world-wide distribution. As a result, the French agency was now back ahead of its rivals on the news front. It beat by nearly fifteen minutes the first reports of the tsunami and earthquke given by its Anglo-American competitors on their world news-wires.

Within two hours of the first news of the tsunami, Hong Kong bureau chief Russell McCarthy, he of the strike-breaking efforts in Paris some nearly two years earlier, had despatched a special envoy to Sydney with orders to proceed to Darwin, and another to Jakarta with orders to head for East Timor.

McCarthy at the same time created a special tsunami news desk in Hong Kong, headed by himself, to handle and coordinate all incoming and outgoing news worldwide concerning the event. Having already beaten its competitors with the first news of the tsunami, France-Dépêches was thereby able to maintain its lead over them thereafter.

This is one of the French agency's early English-language reports of the event:

Giant tsunami swamps Australian coast, East Timor

DARWIN, Northern Australia, 17 July – A huge tidal wave or tsunami, caused by a powerful undersea earthquake, swamped East Timor and the north-west coast of Australia Monday, causing widespread death and destruction.

The tidal wave, which according to eyewitness accounts towered at least 100 feet (32 metres) high, instantly destroyed coastal settlements in regions bordering the Timor Sea north-west of Australia.

Government and humanitarian agencies in Australia and East Timor said it was impossible for the moment to estimate the extent of human casualties and physical damage.

"I don't think we've ever seen anything like this," a spokesman for the Australian coastguard service said. "It looks like whole parts of the coastline have simply disappeared."

A government spokesman in East Timor said entire villages had been swamped or swept away, so that the human toll must be "several hundred at least" but that it was too early to judge further.

Radio stations reported that the wave was seen and felt as far away as Borneo, the Philippines and New Guinea. It was also monitored at the US military base on the island of Guam.

Eyewitnesses on both the north-west coast of Australia and in East Timor said the first wave of water was followed by two or three lesser but still powerful waves.

Naval sources in Darwin said the first giant wave was preceded by a huge fountain or funnel of water above the ocean in deep waters some 200 miles (320 kilometres) from the Australian coast.

Observatories at Strasbourg (France) and Palo Alto (California) estimated the strength of the undersea quake which caused the tidal wave between 8.9 and 9.2 on the Richter scale, making it one of the most powerful ever recorded.

The quake occurred at 1447 hours local time (0547 GMT) off the northern coast of Australia, with an epicentre some 190 miles (300 kilometres) north-west of Darwin, according to the geophysical observatories.

The tsunami story mainly mobilised the Hong Kong news desk and the agency's Asian bureaux and correspondents. But the event was of sufficiently far-reaching impact that a large part of the agency's world network became involved.

As the estimated death toll mounted into thousands and the estimated cost of the damage into hundreds of millions of dollars, came appeals for aid and the organisation of relief work under the auspices of various international and national agencies.

The human death toll was never reliably established – it ranged from 25,000 to 100,000 – due to the fact that mainly small islands and coastal settlements had been hit, and that many of these were relatively undeveloped and poorly mapped.

In truth, the international aid community was already so overstretched by other humanitarian disasters and mounting economic crisis that the response to appeals for help was well short of what was needed. For most of the victims, it was in any case much too late…

* * *

The tsunami story, which held the world headlines for at least a week, was good news for France-Dépêches. Its proficient handling of the event from the point of view of its clients' needs did much to restore the agency's prestige and the professional pride of its journalists, after the crises and failures of recent times.

For its beleaguered management, the tsunami story reaffirmed the French agency's rank alongside Amalgamated Press and Beckers and underpinned its premier position on the Asian news market, where events promised to warm up in the months ahead, notably concerning China, after the agency's own major existential crisis.

The event was a timely reminder that if the Juliet plan or anything like it had been allowed to go through, France-Dépêches might have been so crippled that it could no longer fully rise to such an occasion.

EPILOGUE

Sadly, Russell McCarthy, who had ensured such excellent coverage of the tsunami for France-Dépêches, died soon after the event from a sudden massive heart attack while lunching on noodle soup at his office desk, leaving behind his French wife, Isabelle, and their three school-age children.

His death was another reminder of the unrelenting physical stress of news agency work and the casualties it causes.

Even those who had long borne the brunt of his brusque approach, not to mention his anti-union, pro-management stance, acknowledged his contribution to the collective professional effort – his leadership in teamwork, if you like – that had helped hone France-Dépêches into a major player to be reckoned with in the merciless competitive arena of news gathering and distribution during the agency's first two decades of the twenty-first century.

He undoubtedly thereby helped ensure it a few more productive years.

And so the wheel of fortune turns: some turn with it in time, and some are crushed by it, as by the hand of fate…

This book is printed on paper from sustainable sources managed under the Forest Stewardship Council (FSC) scheme.

It has been printed in the UK to reduce transportation miles and their impact upon the environment.

For every new title that Troubador publishes, we plant a tree to offset CO_2, partnering with the More Trees scheme.

For more about how Troubador offsets its environmental impact, see www.troubador.co.uk/sustainability-and-community